## NO MORE TEARS

"Stay with me, Miranda."

He spoke with intelligence, with sincerity, no hint of pleading. He was a man dealing with the commonsense fact of where and how she was living. If it was true that charity had its roots in the home, then his position was both solid and well grounded. He was simply trying to do the right thing.

Her eyes flickered again. Whenever he spoke, his tone was warm and full, his manner confident without overpowering. The sum total of his being made her feel something indefinable inside, such as a glacier of ice-cracking, a glimpse of some sacred thing revealed. Briefly, she wondered if that glimpse of something sacred was her soul.

A few short hours ago, she'd fallen where she stood. And now, she took a lingering breath of his air, now she was being offered a fresh chance to feel alive again. Did she have one last stand left between herself and suicide? Did she truly want to give up on the living, on herself?

Those were the questions she knew Brody wanted to know. If he knew the answers, he could plot a plan of action to save her. Trouble was, she wasn't afraid of dying. She wasn't afraid to let go.

Maybe that's why he stayed up with her all night, his version of a suicide watch. He had to be tired, even as she was tired herself, and yet never had he abandoned her, no matter how rude she'd been.

"Yes," she said softly. "I'll stay."

# NO MORE TEARS

*Shelby Lewis*

ARABESQUE

BET BOOKS™

**BET Publications, LLC**
http://www.bet.com
http://www.arabesquebooks.com

ARABESQUE BOOKS are published by

BET Publications, LLC
c/o BET BOOKS
One BET Plaza
1900 W Place NE
Washington, DC 20018-1211

All Kensington Titles, Imprints, and Distributed Lines are available at special quantity discounts for bulk purchases for sales promotions, premiums, fund-raising, and educational or institutional use. Special book excerpts or customized printings can also be created to fit specific needs. For details, write or phone the office of the Kensington special sales manager: Kensington Publishing Corp., 850 Third Avenue, New York, NY 10022, attn: Special Sales Department, Phone: 1-800-221-2647.

First Printing: March 2003
10 9 8 7 6 5 4 3 2 1

Printed in the United States of America

*For My Mother, Geri*

# ACKNOWLEDGMENTS

Thank you to the Vera Lewis-Hayes family, whose acreage and history are models for Brody Campbell's lifestyle. I took many liberties with everything I've seen and heard from Lois and Robert Hayes during the research process, but the essential elements of their family heritage—respect for land, honor, and historical pride—are all there. Lois provided me with history on the Abell Community. She also took me on a tour of the area, explaining to me the way black families worked and lived when Abell flourished. Lois is instrumental in tracing and recording the Lewis-Hayes family tree back to the days of the very first Lewis, a man named Freeman Jim who married a woman named Eliza.

I owe a special acknowledgement to Robert Hayes, a man who actually trains horses to run in races around the country. He's a real live Horse Whisperer, and he took the time to answer my questions about those enormous animals, no matter how routine or silly the questions might have been to him.

I must also express heartfelt thanks to Robert's wife, Jo, a retired horse jockey. She was kind enough to read this manuscript in its draft format. Because of her input, I was able to make sure I accurately captured the peace and own-world feel of her family homestead, which the Hayes call, The Farm. From her country home, Jo has a 360 degree view of this rugged Hayes land, of horses grazing, of mothers raising their young, of award winning thoroughbreds who aren't afraid of anyone. I find it awesome to actually know, and include in my family, a woman who once raced horses for a living. From the beginning, I've always admired you, Jo. I'm glad you're my friend.

A special thanks goes to Steve Mize, a detective in the Guthrie Police Department. Steve answered my questions about missing persons protocol as depicted in *No More Tears*. I interviewed him on the inner steps of City Hall during the executive session of a highly volatile city council meeting. He managed to control his surprise at finding himself approached by a romance writer and took my questions seriously. For a minute I thought he might laugh at his predicament, but in the end, he was great about being interviewed. Thanks again, Steve.

Thanks to Johnny Miller and Jim Ham for the idea-inspiring stories they tell in the mornings. I learned about coyotes from them, all sorts of trivia about the weather, about farm machinery, about building homes from the ground up, about gardening, sports, and local politics. I'll forever associate John Deere green with Johnny, white Stetsons with Jim. (John Deere makes top of the line farm equipment.)

I've said it a thousand times and I'll say it again: All my novels are fiction. It's a serious compliment when readers get deep enough into one of my stories to actually feel as if truth instead of fiction is being recorded. I do, very carefully, explore the pleasures in life I adore, such as family unity, peace in my home, food seasoned with love, down-to-the-bone conversations with my girlfriends, gardening because it feels good, book collecting because I can't stop, and the eternal study of the question: What if? Those pleasures are the basis of my writing style.

Kelton Hayes tells me that coups and revolutions begin in coffee houses. This idea fascinates me, as do the coffee clubs circulating through D.G.'s, my husband's coffee shop. For the curious, a coffee club is a group of people who meet at the same time, at the same place, on the same certain day or days of the week. The conversation is stimulating, sometimes unruly, always entertaining.

Special kudos to the following club regulars, people who visit D.G.'s come hell or high water—I'm talking ice storms, snow storms, rain storms, you name it and they've been there. *The Early Morning Crew:* Jim, Johnny, Glenn, Robert, R.C., Les, Darryl, Steve. *The World Travelers Crew:* Dwayne and Rosemary, Perry and Angela, Don and Vela (Don drives a vintage British taxi and a perfectly polished 1935 Austin around town while Vela, a classically trained musician and theater veteran, trains students to excel in music), Tom and Mary Lou, Lon, Ellen, Judy, Philip, Jerry, Shirley, and Kendall. *The Afternoon Crew:* Victor and Dorothy, Corinne, Hazel, Wilbur, Jackie, Betty, Charlene, Imogene. *The Tried and the True Crew:* Woody and Valerie, Gary and Tami, Frank, Holley, Willie, Norma, Tim, and Patty.

Thanks also, to Kelanie Hayes, for making the day run better at the shop. I do a lot of writing between customers at the cash register and she helps me stay on track. Shanna and Mandy—keep doing what you're doing. You guys are awesome.

Thanks Carolyn McHand for sharing your books on 3-D artwork with me and for helping me understand the process. You made it all sound so simple that I felt comfortable writing about it. Thanks to the head librarian at Guthrie High School, Mary Hudson. She allowed me to load up on research material and made me feel welcome. I'll definitely be back. Many thanks to Melody and her staff at the Guthrie Public Library for their amazing support. When I'm on the run, they have my book requests checked out and ready to go before I get there!

I wish to also thank Lisa Sorrell of Sorrell Custom Boots. I adore her work and have learned a lot about the crafting of boots from watching her design material for national shows and competition. Living in cowboy country the way I do, I see a variety of styles and find that I compare every boot to the ones she makes with her bare hands. It's an amazing process. If you're interested in contacting her, she can be reached at lisa@customboots.net.

I've mentioned them before and I'll mention them one more time, as their roles are irreplaceable and unforgettable. Kim and Bobby Lister, Myron and Tamara Lewis because they listened to me and Steve go on and on for years about opening a coffee shop, never doubting we would. Geri

Coleman and Bettye Lewis because their faith in us is relentless.

Our sons, Steven and Randal, who watched us work day after day to conquer our American dream, then live it. Brian and Dee Stevenson who put money on the table and elbow grease on the floors and doors to get the first coffee shop on the Guthrie map. Our business partnership with Brian and Dee bit the dust, but the vision that brought us together in the first place remains true today, chiefly the bond of high goals and total focus.

Dee is not my sister in blood, but my sister in spirit, an artist who crafts one-of-a-kind artifacts she treasures like children who are not for sale: fine porcelain cups filled with tea that never spills, cherubs with painted skin that looks real, Victorian tapestries composed of elegant and regal black women, seamless decoupage, and precision stencil work. Her annual Christmas tree is art that speaks to the artist in me. Her tree takes weeks to go up and months to go down. It bears crystal and china, silver and gold, mini furniture and mini tea sets, music notes and music books, collectible figures, satin pantaloons and other such finery, things that drop my jaw with admiration at one woman's wizardry. Beneath Dee's tree are stories to be told and at her back, is a man who loves her with the kind of devotion money can never buy. She's the first eccentric artist that I know and treasure. Lisa Sorrell is the second.

This book released on my sister's fortieth birthday. Happy birthday, Toni.

In closing, I wish to say that as I rush through the details of life, I do relish its journey, a process best expressed, by this author, through the classic field of romance fiction.

Shelby Lewis
Guthrie, Oklahoma
March 2003

# One

Early June
*Tulsa, Oklahoma*

Miranda Evans couldn't believe it. Leonard, her lying bastard of a husband, was leaving her for another woman. He was handsome—Rick Fox from the Los Angeles Lakers style handsome: The man had soft, wavy black hair going bald on top, high yellow skin that didn't have a blemish to scar it. His perfect white teeth went with his model-perfect smile.

He used his big man's swagger to enter one woman's view after another, but when he married Miranda, she hadn't worried about other women taking over her territory.

She hadn't worried because she believed in fidelity and thought her husband believed in it, too. It took an ultrasound of his unborn child to show her she'd been too trusting. She found the baby's sonogram by accident.

The fact that Leonard kept his long, muscular body honed and fine-tuned in the gym three nights a week should have told her something bad was coming her way one day, this day, but it hadn't told her anything. He didn't just want to look good every minute of the day, he needed to look good. Looking good was a religion with him.

She hadn't wanted common sense to tell her that her marriage was seriously out of order, to do that would mean she'd have to look at the details of her life too hard, too close.

Looking too close meant looking at the why behind Leonard's many obsessions. So what if his nights at the gym got later and later? It made him happy, didn't it? He looked wonderful, didn't he? Damned straight he did.

She'd been much more comfortable and relaxed listening to her handsome husband's baby-you-know-I-love-you propaganda, but all that listening had turned her into a fool. *Fool: person lacking in sense or intelligence.* Fool, as in herself.

There was no way in the world she would ever trust him again, not when he'd made his little-sweet-something-something on the satin sheet side pregnant. Leonard liked sex on satin sheets, even before they married, he'd given her a set.

Had he presented his new lover with the same kind of sheets? Had he? She bet he had. The jerk. Lying son-of-a-gun.

She aimed teary eyes at him and hated herself for crying. There he stood, legs akimbo, arrogant and gorgeous as ever, trying to get her to understand that she was slowing him up.

As far as he was concerned, obstacles were made for knocking down, then forgetting about. His wife was an obstacle, a liability.

Miranda knew he could do it, too, forget all about her. She watched him in action the last seven years of her life, their life. Damn him, damn him for turning her world every other shade of blue: azure, indigo, sapphire, turquoise, aquamarine, cobalt; sad blue, dejected blue, depressed and dispirited blue.

Leonard Evans was going to be a DAD and she knew how important that was to him. He never would have married her if he'd known she wasn't the perfect woman she'd appeared to be, but she hadn't known she wasn't the perfect woman. She hadn't known her body wasn't wired to give birth.

She hadn't known that news of her infertility would be treated as a sin in her husband's hazel-green eyes, those twin optic shields between the well-dressed outer man and the treacherous bastard within.

She became obsessive about keeping her figure in tip top shape for him. She went to the hair salon every two weeks, had her nails done, her feet pedicured—just for him. Always for him.

She bought fresh lingerie and nightwear every other month, bought new clothes during the months in between to keep him in suspense. Her skin was flawless, her manners impeccable, her feelings under pristine control—except when she was painting.

When she painted, she forgot all about him, all about her inability to have his child, something she knew she couldn't change and did her best not to think about, because thinking about it only made her sad.

When she painted, the single focus of her being was to trick the eyes of her customers by getting them to see the flat surface of her murals in three dimensions, trick them into thinking her art was a living, breathing thing. Miranda was all about illusion, Leonard was not.

Maybe that's why he despised her art so much, why he sought to break her concentration by reminding her she wasn't a real woman after all. She'd been saying *I'm sorry* ever since they discovered the melancholy news year three into their disintegrating marriage.

A psychotherapist, Leonard practiced mental healthcare in an upscale downtown building, complete with a deluxe office, meeting room, lobby, and middle-aged secretary. His clients were firmly middle class, usually of dual-income homes, clientele who used his services the way some people used aromatherapy or deep massage as a way to micromanage anger and stress. He said it was a Baby Boomer thing.

He rarely dealt with serious cases of depression or other severe mental illness because he screened his clients carefully before he took them on. In this way, he developed a reputation among his peer group as a designer doctor, a man who preferred short-term, very ordinary cases. Ordinary cases were easy for him to let go at the end of his work day.

He liked his day to be tidy, and that meant working from 7:00 A.M. to 4:00 P.M., Tuesday through Thursday. His weekend began on Friday, Monday afternoons were reserved for paperwork, discussion with his secretary, and the occasional professional meeting. Logical one-two-three order kept his own stress in check. Miranda was the glitch in his life.

She worked Monday through Saturday in an art gallery, part of it open to the public, part of it reserved as her private studio. She specialized in *trompe l'oeil* painting, a form of art that used height and depth perception to make a flat surface appear three-dimensional.

Once used extensively by ancient Romans and Greeks, *trompe l'oeil*, French meaning "deceives the eye," was treasured by Renaissance artists who desired true-to-life windows, ceilings, doors, and other three-dimensional structures. Andy Warhol popularized *tromp l'oeil* with silk screen images. Miranda preferred the Renaissance style.

He didn't like that she painted for a living, a style of work he deemed frivolous, even though she made an excellent living at her craft. Psychotherapy was real work. Painting was a hobby. Hobbies were means of pleasure, unnecessary pastimes such as stamp collecting or gardening.

Miranda had done everything she could to make him happy, everything. In the process, she let him get away with murder. He'd chosen their home, a contemporary townhouse that was all angles and high ceilings.

She wanted a traditional home with full front and backyards. She'd wanted wide, open spaces, nature undisturbed. She'd craved peace, not congestion.

He filled their home with antiques and expensive artifacts, hard furniture, dark greens, dark reds, and Chinese lacquer black. She wanted cozy comfort décor, soft sofas, ottomans, creams and mochas and wines.

He drove a Volvo. She drove a Jeep. He wore suits

to work and slacks to play. She liked casual dresses and relaxed-fit jeans. He liked her hair up. She liked it down. He liked dinner parties and fund-raising events. She didn't.

Determined to salvage an unsalvageable relationship she'd jumped through hoops like a trained dog in a circus act. Things were different now. She couldn't retrieve the lost opportunities, she could only position herself to be ready when new opportunities arrived.

She couldn't let her self-centered husband take another one percent of her life. If she did, it would mean she'd lose her dignity, too. Pride was vanity. Dignity was self-worth. The two did not mix.

Miranda's mind scrambled for a toehold in the mountain she had to climb, this suddenly altered, terribly unknown future. She had honesty. She had dignity. All she needed now was guts. Guts was all about courage, a fortitude of the mind.

It would take guts to salvage her shattered spirit, guts to reinvest in herself, whoever that new self would need to become in order for her to be whole again, secure in her private wants, her ability to achieve them.

At the moment, she didn't know who she was or what she wanted to do besides break Leonard's butt into three disposable parts. He was talking, but she wasn't hearing a word he said. He'd already said more than she could stand. He was leaving her for his mistress, his pregnant mistress, and he was doing it today.

All she could think about as he stood tall above her in his expensive clothes and shining shoes was that seven years of marriage should have been an investment. Seven should have been the seven colors of love, their love.

Seven should have been the seven notes of music in the seventh heaven that was their marriage, and Miranda had been in heaven. Heaven, as in the divine Providence, which, in this case, would have been her residence.

She tried to calm herself, but she was falling apart and they both knew it. As a child, she'd been raised to think she could accomplish any goal, live any dream. Born beautiful, finding and keeping lovers had never been a problem.

Naturally secure, she'd been able to weather marital adjustments, able to adapt and meld her future to her husband's. Not once had she ever imagined that he would betray her, especially for a younger, physically fertile woman. He hadn't been satisfied with a woman who possessed a fertile mind.

Yes, Miranda was crying, but her mind was a red ball of rage. Her harsh, hushed words had the power of a scream. "How could you?"

He glanced at his watch. His eyes shifted. This . . . encounter was taking too much of his time. People paid him to listen. Miranda wasn't part of his program anymore and this encounter was simply a transition point, not a challenge or even an obstacle, just a necessary inconvenience.

"Hey," he said. "I've got to go."

She glanced at his watch, too. It was his Secret Agent Man digital watch by Seiko, and he adored its everyman's look, its unexpected attributes. The

watch was programmed with more than forty greet-
ings. It stored memos and messages, worked as a
stopwatch and a nightlight. It could be viewed ver-
tically or horizontally and was capable of four
different daily alarms.

How many times had she caught him fiddling
with his watch without realizing he used it to juggle
two women? He'd been a secret agent all right. Top
secret. But she wasn't going down without a fight.

"This can't be rushed, Leonard." She left off the
words "you bastard," but they were there in her voice.

Leonard cut another glance at his watch, a muscle
flexing along his left temple as he forced himself to
speak in civil tones. "I want you to move out. Before
the divorce. Tessa's apartment is too small, and this
isn't a good time to sell this place. It's more practical
for you to live in a smaller unit than it is for me. The
baby is going to take up a lot of space."

Miranda snapped.

That's what all this nonsense was about: The B-A-
B-Y. Something, something vital went wild inside
her mind. She wanted to run, to get away from the
man who'd just stolen her future, leaving nothing
in its place.

A baby. A son.

Tessa's baby. Leonard's son.

Leonard just stared at her, this woman who'd
kept his bed warm for the last seven years of their
lives. Just as he knew that she was resourceful as a
rule, that she loved banana splits, dish-rattling
thunderstorms, and novels written by women for
women, he also knew that now, confronted by his
wish to end their marriage, she was crippled with

insecurity. He'd cut the legs from under her, knocked the wind out of her and left her at the side of their emotional road. *Emotion defined as: Agitated passions and sensibilities. Strong, complex feelings.*

Well, he figured, it couldn't be helped. Only his son mattered now. His son. Leonard headed for the front door, never once looking back.

Frantic, Miranda cast her eyes about the house she could no longer stand, the place where every light switch and socket was known by her and her soon-to-be ex-husband. He had access to all the catchall drawers in the cupboards, the stubs of paid bills, scraps of receipts, thumb tacks, rubberbands, pens, and pads of 3" by 3" pink Post-it notes.

He knew that the cups and saucers in the kitchen sink were there for him to wash because it was his turn to wash the dishes. He knew where she kept her slips, her bras, and her panties. He'd seen her first thing in the morning and the last thing at night. He'd known her mentally, carnally, and yet, she was horrified to discover, she hadn't known him.

Hard as she'd tried, Miranda hadn't been able to conceive and he'd used this inability against her. He'd made her feel flawed and unwomanly. He'd made her search for fertility specialists and hoodoo women and miracle cures but in truth, some women were never meant to bear children. She was one of those women.

She bet he wouldn't lie to little miss pregnant Tessa. He would worship her, his newfound goddess, the woman who had given his lying, cheating, handsome self the gift he treasured more than his college degrees, a son, his ticket to immortality.

Damn him. Damn them both.

Hours later, Leonard returned to the home he no longer wanted to share with Miranda. There were European antiques and paintings in each nook and cranny, many of them purchased from Swan Antiques or William Word in Atlanta, Georgia, then shipped to their home in Tulsa. He especially enjoyed collecting console tables, which were shelves attached to a pair of table legs, the entire structure attached to a wall for support.

He liked the tables because they worked as molding for the walls in the same way that strips of carved molding worked for the corners of ceilings by adding depth and character to a wall, and to a room. He had a lovely selection of his version of three-dimensional wall art: French tables with sleek curved legs and a few neoclassical-styled tables with slick straight legs. He enjoyed the tasteful opulence, the refinement, the culture and the class.

There was no way in the world he could let Miranda keep his antique table collection, his wall art, his home. No way. He believed a clean break in a relationship was the best break. All or nothing.

He wanted, needed the best, and for him, the best was Tessa, the mother and keeper of his unborn son, his future: Leonard Junior.

Until Tessa's revelation, Leonard's greatest fear had been dying without a namesake and legal birth heir. He hadn't wanted a child by artificial means, either surrogate or some other medical intervention. That Miranda was unable to conceive had made her flawed in his eyes. Flawed women were not his style.

Her perceived affliction affected his mind, which in turn, affected his point of view; no longer was Miranda the idealistic princess in a fairytale picture book, their marriage. Instead, she was the queen in their fairytale story, no longer the perfect dream-girl, but the beautiful woman, fundamentally and irreparably flawed.

Mirror, Mirror on the wall, who's the fairest of them all? Tessa, that's who. The future Mrs. Leonard Evans. Senior.

He needed that fairytale relationship, and as the ritual prince, he only felt alive when he had his very own Cinderella. Cinderella was grateful, she needed the prince. Cinderella was fertile; she brought those around her to life and, therefore, she was a creator. Cinderella was a homebody. Miranda was not.

He needed his woman at home, not in the art gallery. When he arrived home after a day spent sorting out other people's problems, he wanted to be pampered. He wanted his clothes cleaned and pressed, dinner and fresh flowers on the dining room table.

Many days, Miranda was so caught up in her art, she lost track of time. Leonard, a clock watcher, was paid by the hour, and for him, time was money. It didn't occur to him that all that clock watching made him tense, often bored and dissatisfied with life in general, a deep level of unhappiness that found an easy target and release in his wife.

Unlike Leonard, she moved with time in motion. Rarely did she stop to watch a clock. Instead, she relied on the sun to tell time or alarm clocks to tell her it was time to shift from one activity to another.

He had come to despise this freedom of mind, because it kept her separate and independent of him, definitely not his dream Cinderella. For that dream girl, he'd searched for and found his darling Tessa.

After the baby was born, he'd teach Tessa how to cook his meals with a wok, how to care for his clothes with her own hands, how to maintain his home, his needs, his wants. She wouldn't be interested in running a business, she'd be too busy running his home and raising his son.

In return, he'd treat her the same way he treated his collectible antique consoles, those well-polished and well-dressed artifacts that fit superbly within the setting of his perfect, picture book life with possessive fixation.

He was being gracious by giving Miranda a few days to think about her immediate future, without the pressure of being served papers, without the coldness of a note saying good-bye. He was a real man and real men did their dirty work in person. Telling his wife good-bye forever was extremely dirty work.

He was adept at handling the psychoneuroses of others, their anxieties, their obsessions, their symptoms of physical illness due to mental and emotional strain. He just couldn't do it for himself. At least, not easily or cleanly.

But Miranda wasn't there. He wondered, briefly, about what had transpired when he closed the door behind him that morning.

\* \* \*

The click of the door lock had registered through the blue funk whipped together when Leonard strode out the front door, out of her life, into another woman's arms. She just couldn't stand it. She wouldn't. Her black eyes, robotic, devoid of expression, had scrolled over the living room, his living room, Leonard, Tessa, and Leonard Junior's living room.

750 Wyndham Drive was no longer Miranda's home. Home. Until now, it had been the center of her being, her strength and solace, the springboard for her creative mind. Seven, the cycles of life. Five, the senses of being. Zero, completeness.

The one thing in this horrible scenario she knew for real was that in fairytales, the queen might go down, but she didn't go down easy. Ever. Classic fairytales were dominated by evil deeds and evil doers: child eaters, hairy monsters, and other imminent disasters. In the tales she remembered, the heroines were strong and resourceful. They were the kind of women who knew how to walk forward.

In the bedroom, she'd opened the closet, flicked a glance inside, but touched nothing. Why? Because of Leonard. Leonard had bought those things. She shut the closet door. She didn't need the cropped jackets, the leather trimmed hats, the duster pants sets, the textured skirts, the houndstooth pumps, the animal print dresses— nothing.

She opened the drawers in her expensive dresser. She didn't need all that French underwear, the nylon/spandex hip slips, the twenty-dollar pantyhose in black, always black. She didn't need the jewelry, the pendants, the charms, the dangling earrings, the lariat necklaces, the wave link or mesh buckle bracelets—none of it.

She didn't need any of those things because all those items had been handpicked and presented personally by Leonard Evans. The lying, cheating, son-of-a-bitch.

Miranda had gazed into the dresser mirror. Definitely, she was no child. She'd never been poor, and neither was she the product of a dysfunctional family. If anything, she was the queen in the shattered fairytale of her life.

True to form, she was threatened by the existence of a child, this one unborn, male, and already named by his father, already welcome. In this tale, it was the queen who was banished from home.

But like the queen, she too had magic: art. She would use art to cut a path through the woods her husband had thrown her into, all because he wasn't man enough to be a man to her, the kind of man who would share her sorrow instead of turning their mutual grief into his own personal injustice. Damn him, damn him and leave the tears for some other day. *Survive: To live on. Survivor: One who has lived and will live again.*

Miranda took a single something with her, the magic she worked with her hands, her heart and her mind, the cumulative vision and expression of self that she called art. Art was all about skill combined with cunning, entirely subjective creativity.

This was her life, hers, and if the forest was there

to be dealt with, then deal with it she would, one step and one battle at a time. She too locked the door to 750 Wyndham Drive, only unlike Leonard, she didn't plan on coming back.

# Two

*Logan County, Central Oklahoma*

She was a lone figure in the dark. Her shoulders, small and strong, bore the weight of a bedroll and backpack, both of them quality objects, both colored black and blue. On her feet were sturdy, thick-soled boots, gear designed for use over rough, uneven terrain.

It was mid-October, a Tuesday, and in the distance, the plaintive sound of a traveling freight train was met by the song of free-ranging coyotes. The wild animals spoke to the ragged remnants of the woman's heart, and she answered them with a plaintive cry of her own. The sound was sorrow personified, inarticulate without the use of the normal syllables required to make words.

In this broken place, her mind, she felt no hope, its silvery light far too tarnished for her to ever think it might shine again. Her dreams, now withered and brown, were fantasies she no longer cherished. She had nothing to live for, not even herself.

Her movements mechanical, she halted her cross-country trek. First, the bag on her shoulders, then the bedroll, fell away from their slim perch. The items slid down the backs of her arms, her wrists, and then, to the dry, wind-stroked weeds atop the soil, dense clay soil the color of red.

On her left knee she knelt down, and then she knelt down on the right. Small, irregular stones pressed against the expensive denim of her jeans, but she ignored the pain. The stone-feel of her heart caused the greater agony.

Merciful God, she thought. Merciful . . . God. Her soul, in the night, part whisper, part despair, felt loud in her ears, as if it suddenly had the power of wings and was flying up and away, into a distance too great for her to touch again.

And then she collapsed, not gracefully, but hard, the freefall knocking her breath away. Still, she savored the feel of the dense red clay, the sharpness of the rocks, the cover of darkness. Red was the color of blood, the color of life, and the last of hers was ebbing away. Come death or redemption, she had no place left to go, no place left that felt like home.

Astride his horse, Genesis, Brody Campbell searched his property for rogue coyotes. In recent days, the animals had attacked and killed cattle on neighboring land. The mare and new foal in his round pen required extra protection, hence the loaded shotgun he carried at his side.

Not one to kill for sport, he hunted, like now, only when necessary for the survival of the creatures that relied on the habitat he owned and cultivated—Campbell land.

For close to an hour, he saw nothing unusual; but then, in the distance, his eyes discerned something extraordinary. He blinked once, twice: A body lay crumpled on the ground. The discovery quickened his heart.

Close inspection disclosed the shape of a woman, though she looked more dead to Brody than alive. A coyote attack on a human was outside the norm, but not impossible. As a pack, the animals were fearless.

It was near midnight, the fabled witching hour. Finally, he understood why sleep had eluded him. First the coyote music and now this, this curious mystery in the landscape, this fallen woman in the wrong place at the right time, his place, his time.

A professional trainer, he raised thoroughbred horses for racing. He worked and lived on a farm homesteaded in the 1940s. Passed down to him through three generations, the thousand-acre spread was as much a part of his character as the heirloom saddle between himself and his horse. He dismounted, his intention to provide hope and rescue to the woman who lay before him.

Kneeling, he gathered the stranger's still body to his chest. Using his teeth, he pulled the tips of yellow leather work gloves from the fingers of his right hand. He felt her pulse, steady but faint. Gently, he slid the hair away from her temple, and then Brody did something he never imagined he'd do to a woman he didn't know. He kissed her.

The woman awakened, not by the opening of her eyes, but by the inhalation of her breath. She inhaled a full second before she released. No distressed moan, no stifled scream, just that slow breath and its two second release, and still, her eyes remained closed.

His voice was harsh with leased tension. "Lady," he said, "tell me your name."

"Miranda."

To the count of one, he took a long, jagged breath. To the count of two, he let the breath go. "Are you hurt?"

"No."

"Then, open your eyes."

She did, and it was he who stumbled and fell, he who lost the ability to breathe. This woman, Miranda, bore the eyes of the wounded—shell-shocked, bewildered, tragic in some indecipherable way that perhaps not even time could heal.

For him, time mastered the tempo and composition in the life he lived and loved, a life that now opened itself to the secret fears of a woman in jeopardy, this woman. For a brief few moments, Brody was unaffected by the passing of time, and in this way he experienced timelessness, its scope and power influenced by this lone woman in the dark.

Within this endless realm, the twin senses of touch and sight were both immediate and intense. He stood from his kneeling position, the warm mold of his arms making a cradle for her, the bend of her knees over the crooks of his arms, her head against his shoulder.

But her eyes, sweet Jesus. Her eyes told him the truth she had yet to speak, that she didn't care if she lived or if she died. She didn't care, but he did, and so he strode with her to his black steed, to Genesis, intent on setting her upon the heirloom saddle that he treasured, intent on saving her from whatever had broken her will to survive, even if that meant saving her from herself.

He eased his body into position behind her, a precious cargo he pressed against the wall of his chest. But then, she stilled him with a tone suspended in the netherworld between shadow and light, as if she didn't care if he answered her question or not.

She asked, "Where are you taking me?"

His emotions were indescribable, yet he knew he'd remember the fragrance and feel of her for the rest of his conscious life. His voice was a deep rumble. "Home," he said. "I'm taking you home."

The ensuing silence between man and woman simmered with questions needing to be asked, troubling answers needing to be told; and yet, all was not silent in the night that had called to them both.

The moon was bright, but not full, which made it easy for him to see the owl hooting gently from its perch atop a cottonwood, the ancient tree dying from the top down, a sentinel of time-past and time-present.

A million tree frogs serenaded the horse and its riders, but it was the sound of hooves pounding against the earth that calmed the cowboy's jagged nerves; these were nature-rhythms, trail-riding beats, primal chords to rural born and bred men like him. Nerves in order, he concentrated on the woman resting between the vee of his thighs.

Boneless and trusting, she leaned against him. Though it made no sense to him at all, the wild

nature of the woman caused his heart to catch with
fire and ignite. Wild things thrived without cultiva-
tion or care. Certainly no nurtured woman would
wander alone, in danger, as this woman had.

Something stormy, something turbulent had happened to her. Now she was reckless, fair game to
those who hunted for sport, for food, or for profit.
Fortunately for her, he wasn't that kind of man.

Come morning, he and this stranger would no
longer share this fragile bond of rescued and rescuer.
In the morning, she would leave him. For now, he
felt content to watch the wild beauty as she slept.

Only Miranda was not sleeping. The weather had
shifted in the valley of her mind. No longer cold
and inhospitable, the valley was warm. The warmth
helped her think. Most important, she felt safe.

Far from oblivious to the hazards of her plight,
she was acutely aware the huge stranger had no desire to harm her; he'd had ample opportunity to do
so when he'd found her. His daring and decisive ac-
tions marked him a hero, her hero.

The leather of the saddle creaked as the majestic
horse carried them across the grassy plain. Whatever vista lay in front of her, she had no wish to see
it. Eyes closed, she concentrated on the experience
of refuge and solace inside her hero's arms.

He wore a snug cotton shirt that smelled as if it
had been pulled off a clothesline just moments before. The fresh, old-fashioned scent made her think
of sunshine, clean water, and a soothing breeze.
The softness of the shirt counterbalanced the hard-
ness of his chest. There, the muscles were tough,
lean from constant athletic use.

His arms, equally solid, equally lean were teth-
ered by whatever humanity had driven him to kiss
her natural brown lips. It was the tempered
strength of his mouth and his hands that awakened
her from the depressed stupor in which she'd been
found.

She should have been afraid, but she wasn't.
What she felt was the urge to paint, not about the
physical man but about the sensation of the man,
his presence, his aura, his decisiveness, his . . .
scent.

Within minutes, they arrived at the Campbell
homestead. Once there, Brody felt a stab of uncertainty. For all he knew, she might be a criminal on
the run from prosecution. The only stirring the
stranger had done in his arms was to nestle deeper
into the shelter he'd made for her within the hol-
lows of his body.

In his moment of caution, he searched the details his instinct and subconscious had discerned
about her. She was clean. Her hair smelled like
tropical fruit. Her skin was smooth, soft, and
creamy. She wore no perfume. Her clothes were
quality. She had lots of pockets but the pockets
were empty.

She had no purse, but the backpack she carried
was stuffed and heavy. Her bedroll was a thin sleeping bag, rolled tight. Everything about her was
tight, the slight furrow to her brow, the tension
about her lips, everything.

From her clean and well-kept appearance, the
coldness of her skin upon his first touch, he suspected she had either been let out of a car in this

particular spot, or she'd walked from Guthrie and was headed west to the next nearest city, Crescent. But why?

The sheer mystery of her inspired him to protect her. Whatever lone, internal monster had driven her to the brink of disaster's door had been arrested by his sudden, out-of-the-ordinary appearance. Normally, he didn't worry about coyotes.

Not particularly religious, he'd never given more than an abstract thought to the ideals of destiny and chance. His beliefs were simple; thought before action, truth before mercy, honor at all times, trust that everything wrong will eventually be made right again. For him, time was the ultimate equalizer.

Time set the stage for daily life in the form of morning, noon, and night. It set the era, of which morals were either devised, renewed, or discarded. Time broke the continuum of daily life into manageable bits; from the tick of the clock to the progression of the seasons to the three cycles of human existence: its beginning, its middle, its end.

The one organized act of faith Brody practiced was the art of friendship. Living in a small community, he had a select group of friends he'd known from the first day of elementary school through his last day of high school.

He couldn't afford to brush this small circle of true friends off when he was miffed about something said or done in the heat of a volatile moment. These were the people he called upon any time of day or night for any reason at all, regardless of whether the last time they'd spoken was ten months, ten days, or ten hours ago.

For Brody, the art of friendship began with listening. An active listener attended to the physical details of the speaker as well as the nuances in voice tone. Flickering lashes were noticed, muscle tics and twitches, body tenseness.

Was the speech tight and high pitched or controlled, carefully modulated? Was it open or friendly? And then, there were the words themselves, relaxed and slurred, slang riddled, clipped, abrupt, each syllable enunciated.

Miranda's body language was depressed. Yet, instinctively, she trusted him, the way a mortally wounded animal is able to discern the difference between man intent on killing and man intent on healing.

Her voice had been clipped, controlled, educated. Neither her body language, her words, nor her attitude showed true fright, perhaps, because she was beyond stark fear. He didn't question his decision to bring her home, but he wondered if later, she would. Someone had to be worried about her, someone, somewhere, but who?

They reached his home.

Brody slid off Genesis, the wild thing still in his arms, when his ranch hand, Duke, separated himself from the varying degrees of darkness from which he'd watched his boss approach.

In his seventies, Duke Ransaw was the kind of man who lived best when he belonged to no one, the kind of man who needed a job without someone looking over his shoulder, a bed without a regular bedmate, so that he didn't have to explain to a woman where he was going or when he was coming back.

The old man spoke without inflection. For the moment at least, what Brody did this night was Brody's business. Anything else could wait until morning. "I'll put Genesis up for you. Lillian'll take care of the rest."

For the first time since spying Miranda on the ground, Brody relaxed. This was home and his home was his heart, his sanctuary. His gaze slid from the live-and-let-live look on Duke's face to the foundling who struggled in his arms. Alarm gripped him. Her eyes, sweet God in Heaven, her eyes were empty chambers with no hope and no soul.

"Put me down," she rasped.

"No."

As if by magic, the front door of Brody's rambling old home opened, and a pool of warm light enchanted the lost woman, invited her, welcomed her. In response, she did more than live in the moment, she took a peek at the future, and stepped inside.

# Three

Miranda became aware of her surroundings in a way she hadn't been aware of them until she'd slipped off Brody's horse. The front room she entered was spacious, decorated in shades of mocha, burgundy, and cream.

The overall scheme was restful, welcoming, and warm, as was the expression on the woman's face who studied her in the way one might study a wounded animal on the verge of running wild.

The woman read Miranda's intent exactly. She did want to run, not because she was afraid, but because the woman who watched her so carefully made her want to be held in her arms, held in the soothing way loving mothers hold the children they treasure.

Miranda desperately wanted to be held with care, it's why she'd chosen not to resist the stranger. His arms had been wonderful around her, the sound of his heart beating against her ear, an ancient melody that soothed the edges of her own self-neglect.

The woman said to Brody, "Give her to me."

Those words broke the trance Miranda had been under. This was no fairytale, no fantastic story of magic, myth, and lore. She wasn't out of her mind with worry or fear. Physically, there was nothing wrong with her at all. It was her soul that was broken, not her mind. This wasn't a dream she was living. This was for real.

"You people can't keep me here."

The woman wasn't disturbed at all. She looked intrigued. "Honey, there's something about you that speaks to the mama in me. Besides, I've never been one to mind my own business. No reason to start minding it tonight."

Some nameless emotion shook Miranda from the inside out. Her voice was laced with it, heavy with it, and she thought, perhaps, that nameless emotion was desire. The desire to belong, to be wanted, to be . . . loved. It was irrational, she knew, to feel this way so soon.

"I'm a private person," she said, as if reminding herself it was true, not them. "I'm very private."

The elder woman waved a careless hand in the air. It was a strong hand, a wide hand capable of managing errant children, or grown women with troubled eyes. "Roaming around on *private* property in the middle of the night ain't a normal thing to do, honey. Besides all that, I'm nosey, like I said."

"But—"

"Come here, girl."

Miranda had allowed herself to be kissed by a dark stranger, to then be carried away by him into the night, and now she allowed this full-figured woman to draw her into an embrace that shook her composure to the core.

She felt like an abandoned child who'd been swept up and held tight by a woman who believed

NO MORE TEARS 41

in following her heart. But then, this was a country woman, the type of woman who didn't think it was unusual to be kind to strangers.

Yes, it was desire Miranda felt, a tangled knot of longing that found solace in the company of people she'd never met, inside a home that smelled of fresh cinnamon and hot apples. Somehow, she'd found a sort of paradise.

Pressed against the soft round comfort of the woman's chest, Miranda let more of her guard down. Once done, she committed an act she hadn't been able to pull off since leaving Wyndham Drive, she cried.

Hers were not silent tears of hopelessness, rather they were tears reflecting the change in mood flowing inside her. Brody's insistence upon helping her had forced her to reconnect her thought process with her emotions.

The reconnection was the tears. The tears represented her flow in these new events in her life. Being in this home, with these kind people, in the dark of night was all about opportunity, the chance to begin a new page in life. She wasn't sure she was ready.

On the red clay soil, she'd been beyond tears, emotions not part of her lifestyle anymore. In order to cry, one had to feel, even if all one felt was self-pity. Until her rescue, Miranda felt nothing, not one thing, and now, Brody was there to pull her away from the madness. It was he who brushed her tears away.

"Don't," he said. "Don't do it."

Lillian hustled him out of the way, one arm still

wrapped around Miranda. "Crying lets the bad out. This is good."

Miranda stood motionless. She wasn't tired. She wasn't scared. She wasn't lonely. She was exactly as Brody had found her, indifferent to herself, even as she was conscious of the new page she'd been dealt. She had no goals. She was not important. She had no desire to win anything or to fight anyone.

She was alive because physically, she was healthy. In primordial terms, she was a living organism making its way through the ecosystem until it died on its own or was killed. At this point, the relationship she trusted best was the connection between her body to its immediate environment—this room, this moment.

She'd stopped running off emotion when she left Leonard in Tulsa. In this regard, she truly was a wild thing, only she didn't run with a pack. To run with a pack meant to conform, something she never intended to do again.

Yes, the tears marked a transition from the place she'd been only moments before, but they were not tears of joy, or relief: She was beginning to feel again, a sensation similar to heat warming ice-cold feet. She remained neutral in face and attitude, oblivious to the reaction her presence caused in the people who flanked her.

She did not recognize her affect on them, but it would have surprised Miranda to realize that she, with her scarcely blinking black eyes, scared the hell out of them. They wanted to fix her, but they didn't know how.

Lillian kept on holding her, until the tears

turned from something uncontrollable to something almost pleading in nature. This was a young woman trapped in some harsh reality that found its release through these bitter tears. It was like a mannequin crying. Or a robot. True and false mixed together.

Miranda's inner doors were opening, but she wanted to keep them closed. Closed doors meant she had less baggage to handle every day. Trouble was, the baggage was heavy. She was tired, the reason she'd sloughed her bedroll, her backpack, in order to lie down, perhaps forever. Only forever hadn't come, Brody had.

In turn, he wanted to hurt whoever had hurt her, this woman covered with mental don't-touch-me thorns. Certainly, before him stood a shell of a human being. He wracked his brains to figure out a way to help.

"Lillian," he said.

"Yes?"

"Guest room ready?"

Lillian gave him an oh-please look. "Always."

To Miranda she said, "Come on, now, honey-girl. Things always look better in the morning and morning is just about here."

To this, Miranda laughed, softly. The sound was as hollow and rootless as the eyes she used to guide her from one room to the next.

In minutes, Lillian returned to the living room. She found Brody pacing. "You all right?"

"No."

"I'll be heading to town tomorrow as planned, but I'm gonna check in with you in case you need me. Ain't but a few minutes drive between here and there."

"I know."

Lillian glanced at the clock: 2 A.M. "Calling the sheriff?"

"Not yet."

"Brody, honey?"

He had the look of a man cast in stone. Deeply masculine in design. Sculpted physique. Devoid of expression. "Yeah?"

"Be careful."

His gaze followed her eyes to the hallway, then to the bedroom beyond it. "Why? You think she's dangerous?"

"Only to herself," Lillian said. "I'd swear somebody must have beat the crap out of her only there are no marks to be seen. I know because when I gave her one of your T-shirts to sleep in for the night, she changed clothes in front of me as if I was furniture or something. As if she was nobody. But when I left the room, she thanked me."

Brody spoke as if he voiced an afterthought instead of the mantra it really was, the mantra that hadn't stopped playing in his mind since discovering Miranda: *How did she get here? How did she . . . ? How did . . . ? How . . . ?*

"What could bring her to her knees like that, Lillian? A woman like her?" A clean, articulate woman, a gorgeous woman. Mysterious.

"Sorrow. It's grief we feel from that girl. I think it was you who found her because you were supposed to find her, just like tomorrow I'm heading off to town for three weeks because I'm not supposed to be here while you work your magic with her the way you do those antsy horses people bring you to calm down. Know what I'm thinking?"

"What?"

"I'm thinking it's not a woman's touch she needs."

Brody eyed her with love and incredulity. She'd watched Robert Redford in the film *The Horse Whisperer* and turned it off because the hero in the story didn't hold a candle to him when it came to taming skittish equine flesh.

He trained horses in real life and was considered by his peers to be an expert in his profession. He'd learned his craft from veteran men in the race-horse industry, and from the best man of all, his own father.

He said, "You talk like some old conjure woman."

Lillian smiled. "It's called age and wisdom, sugar. That woman's tears mean there's still something in her to work with. I'm talking about hope here." She patted him on the shoulder, then gave the bone a little squeeze. "I'm gonna catch a few hours or I won't be any good tomorrow. Get some sleep, too, if you can."

Brody watched her retire to the cottage out back, located down a brightly lit walk edged in white iceberg shrub roses, the only flowers on the property that weren't growing wild. He intended to put the roses in a small vase in the guest bathroom for Miranda to see in the morning. The buds were small, but smelled delightful.

Just as he entered the hallway, she opened her bedroom door, fully dressed. He didn't mean to glare, but he did it anyway. "What are you doing?"

Her gaze shifted to the flowers crushed between his fingers. It was long after midnight and yet he didn't look tired. With him standing there, bouquet in hand, it might have been midafternoon during a social visit between a courting couple. "I don't know you people."

"We all know good things when we see them. Nothing has been done to hurt or alarm you here."

"Where am I? Exactly."

"A long way from home."

She laughed, a small desperate sound that raised the hair on Brody's neck. He was tempted to go for Lillian, in case Miranda was breaking down mentally, but there was strength in her still, there, in the erect way she held her body, as if not even the wind could knock her down if it tried. But something had, Brody thought. Something had made her lie down to die.

For him, the middle son in a trio of male children, a man raised by his original parents in the only home he'd ever known, among friends and neighbors he trusted, Miranda was a puzzling paradox.

She was a disturbed personality in an unusual situation, a woman who trespassed in the middle of the night to music scored by people-savvy coyotes, a woman with contradictory emotions, the cynical versus the distressed. Who was she? What was she? How could he let her go?

He had lived his entire life in Logan County. He knew all its major players and their agendas. Miranda belonged to no one, of this he was certain. So why was she so desperate to escape now when she'd been so docile only moments before? Was she afraid to be in the house alone with him, now that Lillian had said good-bye for what was left of the night?

In two strides Brody entered Miranda's space. "I promise you this, come morning, I'll help you get back home. No matter where home is."

Her top lip curled at the idea of home, or maybe her lip curled at the idea he would somehow assist her. He didn't know. He did know that in her displeasure were secret, sad memories, bitter memories. In her curled lip was a stiff measure of disgust with some hate thrown into it. "I have no home."

He didn't miss a beat. "Then, stay here."

Her top lip straightened, as did her shoulders when she squared them off. Although she had been saved, she hadn't asked for a savior. She hadn't been in search of a miracle when he'd come along. Not consciously, anyway. "Why?"

He leaned a fraction forward. "Why not?"

Cryptic flickers of things past and things present flashed through her mind. Her wedding day. The bracelet Leonard's mistress had left for her to find on her marital bed, its discovery the key to Pandora's box. The ultrasound of Leonard's baby, the one which cemented the final breakup of their busted marriage. A determined man named Brody.

She perused the length of him. Whatever she saw, she liked, especially his even, dark brown skin, the slight stubble on his face, eyes as black as her eyes, strength greater than her strength. This was a man, a real man, and she liked his do-right message.

But what were his imperfections? They had to be there, if not naked to the eye, then definitely under the skin. He had to have bad habits, unfinished projects, people he'd been meaning to call but had never found the time. The man, being human, had to be flawed, somewhere, some way, but she was hard pressed to find a chink in his armor.

Where once she would have trusted him on face value, she now looked for another face behind the face being offered. Leonard had done this to her, screwed around with her system of trust.

At this moment, she hated Leonard Evans, hated herself even more for the solitary, distrusting woman she'd become. In damning him, she'd damned herself, for certainly there was no pleasure in revenge.

She released some tension. "No wife, Brody Campbell? Kids? Girlfriend?"

"No on all three counts."

A man this too good to be true had to have a woman who wanted him all to herself. He was a knight who didn't realize that chivalry was dead. And yet, it was his chivalry that caused her skin to tingle, as did the sound of his voice, his see-through-you intensity.

If he tried to eat her alive, she wouldn't have the will to fight him. Suddenly, she wanted to feel hot with passion again, wanted to rejoice in her femininity, right now, held tight in this cowboy's arms. There had to be a woman in Logan County who felt the same way she did. There had to be. Men like him were for keeps.

"Why is it no," she asked, "on all three counts?"

His eyes narrowed a fraction. How could she banter with him? And he with her? "This is stupid. Standing in the hall. Me holding flowers like I'm some kid, which I'm not. And you," he paused to gather himself, "you're dressed to walk out of here without telling anybody good-bye."

"All true."

She stared into the most honest, determined face she'd met since making her way across the state, mostly on foot. She wondered what her true reason for leaving was when she'd been saved, then made to feel welcome.

Yes, the scene was ridiculous, silly because she was behaving in a selfish, ungrateful way—Leonard's way. Even though she knew she was wrong, she couldn't seem to stop herself from pushing Brody away.

She said, "I have no money to trade with you."

Brody was ten times the man Leonard had been. He was deeply insulted she brought the subject of money up at all. Some petals on the flowers were not only crushed in his fist, but bruised. "None is required."

She should have been nervous, with his body blocking her exit, his shoulders filling the hallway, his attitude steeped in leashed anger. But her skin was all tingly, her senses were in high gear. It was after 2:00 A.M., but she didn't care. She lived with time, not against it.

So she pushed his envelope, pushed to see how far she could go before his beast came out. It was there wasn't it? Tired and edgy about the edges, he was bound to lose his chivalry, but his kindness never once wavered. She must be mad, crazy mad, to refuse them both the sleep they needed to get by.

"I suppose," she said, "you want an explanation."

Of course he did. "It's only natural that I want to know why you think so little of yourself."

She trusted him, yes, based on his honesty and kindness, but there was something she wanted to understand. What was it about him that turned her so inappropriately on? Was it the way he met the challenge of her negative attitude?

There were as many questions she wanted to ask him as he wanted to ask her. She started with the question that had inspired her to get dressed all over again. It had been his T-shirt she'd been wearing. It smelled like him, fresh and clean.

"Why did you kiss me?"

His head tilted to one side, his gaze lighting on her hair, her face, her skin. "If I knew the answer to that, Miranda, I could explain why I'm arguing with a stranger in the hall of my home when I should be dead asleep."

Over the roses, the two eyed each other, the scent of honey between them. Suddenly, the air had a wonderful static in it, wonderful in the way of finding a wild flower living in a place where it didn't belong.

"The roses are beautiful," she said. "They really shouldn't be blooming at this time of year, but the weather's been so nice, I guess you guys got a late fall showing."

Her smile eclipsed real time. For Brody, she was every myth he'd ever heard about a damsel in distress. His Sleeping Beauty. His Cinderella. Her eyes were glossy black, no beginning or end to them, fathomless. He reached for her hand and she took his.

"I get the idea we won't be going to sleep," he said.

"No."

He squeezed the hand he held. "How does hot chocolate sound?"

"Delicious."

He led her into the kitchen. He pulled a chair out for her at the table. He put the flowers in a drinking glass and put the glass next to the napkins at the table's center. All was silent as he boiled water in the blue kettle that was always on the back burner. He took two mugs from a cupboard. He filled the mugs with the cocoa mix Lillian made herself and kept on the counter in a decorative red tin.

He spoke over his shoulder. "Marshmallows or whipped cream?"

"Neither. Thank you."

He sat across from her at a table made of solid oak. He tried to put her mind at ease. "I live here alone for the most part."

"What about the elderly couple?"

"Duke has been here longer than I have, and I was born right here in this house. He's family, friend, and mentor."

"Siblings?"

"Two brothers."

"What about the woman?"

"Lillian is a friend of my mother's. When she wasn't able to keep regular hours anymore, my mother offered her a live-in position here."

"She's in the house right now?"

"No."

"I'm surprised."

He quirked a brow. "Because we're by ourselves?"

"Yes."

"Duke lives in an apartment above the barn. He cares for the animals and oversees the property. Lillian manages the house for me and lives in a cottage out back. The two of them are my peace of mind. I can travel or work elsewhere all day and not worry about how things are being managed here. Without them, it would be tough to get away at all. The horses keep me fully occupied."

Miranda stirred the chocolate in her cup. "She said she's going to town tomorrow. Would that be Guthrie or Crescent?"

"Guthrie. My parents have a small bungalow there. Mom wanted to live closer to her friends and church, and Dad said this place was more than he needed, so they left me in charge. Plus, my oldest brother's wife runs a coffee shop in Guthrie. It's called D.G.'s. My mother is crazy about her. She likes to help her during the lunch rush. Both of my brothers left the farm right after high school. I stayed here."

"Never been tempted? To leave I mean?"

"Beyond traveling, yes. I've been to twenty of our states already and plan to see the rest before traveling abroad."

Miranda had a hard time imagining the next hour let alone a long trip. "So in essence, you're a confirmed bachelor?"

"Quaint term, but no, not really. It's just that my life is pretty full and I'm not looking for anyone special."

Her smile was guarded. "Another way of saying I'm safe with you."

"I'm not saying anything of the kind. At this point, safety isn't an issue. Even though you're with strangers, you're in a superior position to where I found you. I honestly don't feel we need to discuss the personal security thing again. At this point, it's irrelevant. It's been hours since you came home with me, Miranda. You refuse to rest, which means I won't get any rest, either."

"You don't trust me?"

He gave her a you've-got-to-be-kidding look. Definitely she had plenty of gumption left in her. "Why should I?"

That clearly struck a nerve. Her eyes flashed fire so fast, he almost missed the light. "What do you want to know?"

"Everything," he said. "Tell me everything."

She sipped her cocoa.

"Talk to me, Miranda."

She put her cup down on the table. She put her hands in her lap. She stared straight into his face. She said nothing.

Using a voice as soft as the one he'd use with a filly delivered to him from some troubled place, he prompted her with a smile. "Let's start with your last name."

"Evans."

"Where are you from originally?"

"I prefer to deal with today."

"And for us," he said, "today began at midnight. Literally."

"It did."

"Give me the basics."

This time, it was she who lifted her brow in sarcasm. "As in name, rank, and serial number?"

He fingered the handle of his mug, but didn't raise it to his lips. "Right."

"I'm twenty-five."

He was determined to stay calm. "Where is your family?"

"That part of my life happened before midnight."

Deep lines furrowed his forehead. Their conversation was going nowhere. "You won't talk about your past, then?"

"No."

"Tell me if I'm wrong. You're homeless, friendless, and stubborn."

She almost smiled, almost. She understood quite well the predicament she was in, the puzzle she presented. She was discovered in a state of menace, alone in the dark, without shelter, prey to men and other strange animals, the sound of coyotes around her. Now she found herself isolated again, but this time, she was alone in a house of strangers, a house surrounded by acres and acres of land, with no other neighbor for miles.

She was in this position because she'd chosen to leave her husband, an act that might be construed as a poor judgment on her part. In her heart, she didn't think so. By leaving Leonard, she'd become a true woman of mystery.

A woman of mystery could go anywhere, be anyone. The less she said about herself, the harder it was for Leonard to find her, for him to get his divorce.

Screw Leonard. He didn't make her world go around anymore. She did.

But now, there was Brody. As the master of this secluded house, he was the true hero of this long, event-filled night. She studied him intently. He looked as if he wanted to shake the truth from her.

Let him shake her if he thought it would do any good. Let him. As far as Miranda was concerned, she was a woman without a family, a woman without a past, a woman who answered to no one. Screw Brody, too. This was her life, not his.

She said, "That's about right."

Unexpected anger gripped his mind. "Is there anyone looking for you?"

"Probably."

He tried a different tactic. "Are you running from the police?"

"No."

On impulse, he snagged her backpack from the floor where her jacket lay beside it. If she was worried about his sudden aggression, she didn't show it to him. He felt she should be edgy. He wanted to slash away at her facade. He wanted to . . . drag her across the table and kiss her again.

Before daylight came, he might do just that, kiss her. In anger, he unzipped the backpack. He dumped its contents on the kitchen table. His stare challenged her to confront him for his breach of trust, his sudden meanness.

She lifted the cocoa to her lips. She inhaled its aroma, sipped her drink, and put the mug down. Her expression did not change. She did not speak.

Brody's pulse spiked two levels. What did he see

here? What? Paints. Brushes. Cleaning solvent. Rags. Sponges. Latex gloves. Plastic containers. A well-dressed homeless woman who couldn't sleep, who cried like a robot, a woman with a steady pulse and dark, tragic eyes.

What did he see? Paint stained fingers on her right hand. He opened her bedroll. A change of clothes. Underwear. Socks. A toiletry bag. A minimalist woman who traveled alone, who didn't carry a purse.

He opened the blue canvas toiletry bag. Toothbrush. Toothpaste. Soap. Deodorant. Lotion. Tissue. Comb. Map. A list of names, cities, and telephone numbers. A woman with secrets. A woman who needed him.

He put everything away. There was no hurry. She wasn't going anywhere. He stacked her belongings neatly in one corner of the kitchen.

Her stare was unwavering. Cold. She sipped the last of her cocoa. It was the perfect distraction. She had a task to occupy her hands and mind while Brody considered his next step in dealing with her.

He stared right back. "I've seen your work."

Her head nodded slightly, once. "I thought you looked familiar."

"You painted a mural on my oldest brother's wall. It's beautiful."

"Funny," she said. "While you were ransacking my things, I noticed your resemblance to him. To Jason. It's in the bones of your face, the shape of your shoulders. Something about the way you move."

He knew it would catch up to him later, the lack of sleep, but right now, Brody didn't care about the responsibilities daylight would impose upon him. At this moment, Miranda Evans was his universe.

"My brother told me he hired an itinerant artist to paint a 3-D mural on his dining room wall. I thought he was being extravagant."

"Yes," she said. "For his wife."

"Roanna."

"Yes."

"You didn't walk all the way from their house on Coffee Creek Road, did you?" He looked appalled.

She stretched a bit, like a cat. "What I did yesterday was yesterday."

He studied her intently. His sister-in-law's new mural was a garden at the height of the midsummer season, three-dimensional, rich in color, so alive in texture and content that anyone residing in the dining room, at its table, would feel as if he or she dined on a balcony festooned in midsummer's finest flower glory.

And Jason Campbell, Brody's eldest brother, had hired Miranda on the spot, based solely on first impression, followed up by impeccable recommendation from satisfied clients, and Jason's own desire to give his wife a ten-year wedding anniversary present she would treasure for the rest of her life.

"My brother said he was worried you wouldn't be able to finish the mural before his wife returned from her business trip, but you did. Roanna wanted to meet you, thank you personally, but you'd taken the money and run, to parts unknown."

"Until now," she said.

"Yes," he said. "Until now."

Miranda spoke softly. "You can't stay awake forever you know. Eventually, I'll be gone."

She was right and they both knew it, but Brody wanted her here, today, this night, and the day after. He didn't question his motives for wanting her near him, he just did, and for now that was enough. "Stay with me."

She laughed then, and the sound was reckless. "I don't even know you."

"You stayed in the spare room at Jason's house. Stay in mine, the room Lillian took you to after you got here."

"I want to be left alone," she said. "Let me be."

He didn't care if it didn't make sense or not, but he couldn't do that, leave her alone. "Lillian is leaving in a few hours. I want you to paint something on her walls while she's gone. Surprise her with a garden."

Her eyes flickered. In mockery or humor he didn't know, would never know, because this was a woman who did what she damned well pleased, and it pleased her to stare him to the ground.

It amazed him that she wore no wedding ring. Someone as beautiful and talented as she would certainly be seriously courted. He scrambled for some way to get her talking about herself. "How long have you been on the road?"

Her eyes flickered, he noticed, definitely with humor. This, along with the tears, spurred him onward with his quest to detain her, even though he had no right to do so. He doubted he'd ever meet another woman like her. The time to consider trespass had come and gone the moment he carried her off on his horse.

Still, it was hard to imagine her being so alone in the world, a woman too well maintained to be a true derelict in society. But that was definitely the case, that she was a vagrant, an outcast, a woman without a home. He couldn't stand it, her not having a home when he lived alone, with room to spare.

He found himself selling himself. "I train race horses for a living, which means I'm out of the house most of the day. As I understand it from Jason, you live on-site for room and board in exchange for your 3-D artwork."

"Correct."

"What Jason didn't know is that in between jobs, you're a wanderer."

"Brilliant deduction," she said without inflection. "I'm impressed."

Soon it would be dawn, sunrise. If he didn't do something radical, come morning, she'd be gone again. This thought caused a wrenching sensation in his heart. He ran with his instincts. "Stay with me, Miranda. At least for three weeks."

She didn't say a word.

"It's not as if you have something better to do."

He spoke with intelligence, with sincerity, no hint of pleading. He was a man dealing with the commonsense fact of where and how she was living. If it was true that charity had its roots in the home, then his position was both solid and well grounded. He was simply trying to do the right thing.

Her eyes flickered again. Whenever he spoke, his tone was warm and full, his manner confident without being overpowering. The sum total of his being made her feel something indefinable inside, such as a glacier of ice-cracking, a glimpse of some sacred thing revealed. Briefly, she wondered if that glimpse of something sacred was her soul.

A few short hours ago, she'd fallen where she stood. And now, she took a lingering breath of his air, now she was being offered a fresh chance to feel alive again. Did she have one last stand left between herself and suicide? Did she truly want to give up on the living, on herself?

Those were the questions she knew Brody wanted to know. If he knew the answers, he could plot a plan of action to save her. Trouble was, she wasn't afraid of dying. She wasn't afraid to let go.

Maybe that's why he stayed up with her all night, his version of a suicide watch. He had to be tired, even as she was tired herself, and yet never had he abandoned her, no matter how rude she'd been.

"Yes," she said softly. "I'll stay."

# Four

Miranda woke to the sound of hooves pounding against the earth. She gazed beyond the bedroom window to see Genesis leading several horses at a run across Brody's property. Head high, tail flying, the magnificent male quarter horse led the way. Dogs followed the small herd, attempting to stop them.

She wished she had a camera to record the view, this scene that could easily be straight from a western action film. Only this wasn't a glamour movie of the mythic cowboy, this was real life, and Brody Campbell was a real cowboy. By the grace of God, she was alive to bear witness.

A battered white Chevy, circa 1980, sped to the house. It was Duke Ransaw. He hollered for Brody to come on and hurry up. They had horses to catch.

Miranda kicked into action. She threw on her clothes, left her room at a dead run, and collided with Brody. "Oh," she said. "Excuse me."

"No problem."

He was bare from the waist up, muscles rippling, body hard, nipples raised. His jeans were worn and tight, the top two buttons open. His navel, exposed, was flat and round. She swallowed hard. "The horses."

"I know."

She trailed him into the yard. "What are you gonna do?"

He whistled.

To her amazement, Genesis made a complete u-turn. The other horses followed. Duke took the lead, backed up by the dogs, a motley crew of three mixed breeds.

"Slick," she said.

"Yeah."

In unison, they returned to the house, he with his ripped bare chest, she with her skinny brown feet. The air was cool, tension between them a sheer high wire that required careful navigation to cross.

She'd never seen a half naked cowboy in mostly buttoned jeans and dirty-as-hell work boots before. She wanted to paint him on the wall, an image of horses running in the distance, the sun climbing the sky, crows cawing from the large cottonwood, light blue morning glories on the verge of closing until they opened their petals again at dusk.

She couldn't paint him on the barn wall the way she wanted to paint him if she left after breakfast the way she'd planned. If she left.

Lillian smiled from her position on the porch. She'd seen the horses run off more than once before. Genesis had figured out how to lift the latches to the stalls in order to let his buddies out. "Coffee is going. Breakfast is in the works."

Miranda took note of what she'd merely glimpsed when she first arrived. Lillian was of average height, ample of body, with an hourglass figure at age sixty-two. She wore soft slacks, a fitted tank top, and a lightweight knit jacket, all a becoming shade of lavender. Her hair was gathered in a smooth chignon at the nape of her neck. Her skin, a pretty cinnamon color, glowed with health.

Lillian's eyes sparkled as Brody headed to his bedroom to put on the rest of his clothes. Her smile welcomed their guest. "I gather you two were up pretty late."

Miranda took a full three seconds to answer. "Yes."

"He looks frazzled."

"I'm sorry."

"Don't be. He's a good man. Like many good men who've got most everything they need, Brody's complacent. You've shaken him up a bit. Stirred the pot."

"You don't—" Miranda stopped, not wanting to be rude.

"Spit it out."

"You don't act like a housekeeper."

Lillian made a face that said, *Give me a break.* "Mother hen. Den mother. Cook. Nursemaid. Hostess. Yes, I'm the housekeeper, too."

Miranda inhaled the scent of coffee and felt her stomach purr. Still, she was more curious than hungry. "You're very secure."

"Honey, truth is always best. Like you for instance. What's the truth about you, I wonder?"

"You're right. You don't mind your business."

Lillian's smile was a cross between pleasant and a fraction too cool. "Maybe it's because none of my business is a secret."

Brody joined them in the kitchen, fully dressed. His eyes missed nothing. Instead of drinking from

Lillian and Miranda's witches brew, he straddled the fence of social grace rather than step into their gently boiling feminine waters. "Food smells good." It beat talking about the weather.

Miranda preceded him to the table. "If you came to diffuse the situation," she said, "the situation is diffused."

Before he could respond, Lillian did. "So, you've still got fire, little miss wild child. There's hope for you yet."

Miranda fought back, not realizing she was being baited into fighting for her life. "I didn't ask to be rescued. I don't need to be saved."

Lillian flicked the young woman with a glance that saw everything twice. "You didn't resist the rescue and the fact you're still here tells me you're here for a reason. There's no need to run away and there's no need to play games."

"I don't run away from my problems, or play games."

"No, you just try to disappear."

Miranda felt her pulse kick up a few beats. "Lady," she said, "you've got way too much nerve."

"And you've been on your own too long. Look at yourself, girl. What are you? Twenty-five? Twenty-six? You're clean, yes, but you're wearing the same clothes you had on yesterday, and yesterday Brody found you face down in the dirt."

Miranda's eyes flashed. Her nostrils flared. Her fingers curled into fists, then released. She thought about packing her few things up but knew Lillian had hit the nail on the head. She had nowhere to go.

She thought about disappearing again, but really, for all intents and purposes, she didn't exist. She carried no personal identification. She had no permanent address. All she had was her art and her secrets. "Your opinion is irrelevant."

"So you say."

"That's right."

Lillian laughed, apparently as delighted with Miranda's spunk as she was delighted with Brody's consternation. "You'll do just fine, young lady. Just fine."

Brody recognized what Lillian was doing, the reason he let her conversation with Miranda run its course. He added his two cents to Lillian's cause. "You're probably wondering about all the horses."

Miranda allowed herself to be diverted. She didn't like to fight, not like this when there was nothing critical at stake. Her stay here was temporary. It didn't matter if she was here three months, three days, or three hours. When she was ready to leave, no one could stop her. "Yes."

"I train them to race. Mostly thoroughbreds."

She was intrigued by the picture in her mind. "Kind of like Robert Redford in the movie *The Horse Whisperer*?"

"Something like that. Basically, I use a nonviolent approach to training horses to work with people and to compete with other horses on a professional racetrack. I don't break their spirit. I don't hit them. I connect with them through tone of voice, touch, and patience."

"Love conquers all, right?"

He wondered if her cynicism was a shield. If so, he

hoped it was brief. The last thing he wanted to deal with, on a daily basis, was a smart aleck. Everyone had something to learn from someone else. At least they did in his book of knowledge. For now, Brody was willing to play the get-to-know-you game her way.

He said, "Right."

Lillian rose from the table, a satisfied expression on her lightly powdered face. "I'm hitting the road. Call me if you need me. Miranda?"

"Yes?"

"Stay. At least for a little while."

Miranda said nothing.

Several minutes ticked by as Brody absorbed the air around her. The air still felt cool, but was heating up. He tasted coffee, all sugared and creamed, on his tongue, and knew that Miranda's coffee would taste black and sweet, as she'd only added sugar from the ceramic bowl on the table now set casually for two. Lillian was as transparent as a crack in one of the cupboards.

Emotion took hold of his mind, erasing whatever common sense he had left. Maybe that's what Lillian could see, his fascination, and she was, by word and deed, giving Brody her blessing in the form of a green light. She didn't have to leave right away.

The fact she felt comfortable about leaving Miranda unsupervised in the house while she continued her plans was a great sign of faith that all would be well in the long run. Brody didn't solicit or require her blessing to do what he felt was right to do in his own house, but her acceptance of his decision to help Miranda cheered him. Lillian wished to help her, too.

"I want to be with you, Miranda." The words were out before he could stop them, bold words, true words, words spoken in a harsh tone of voice.

Instead of slapping him the way he thought she might, she said, "I know."

Brody couldn't think of an appropriate thing to say next. His honesty hadn't scared her, but it had scared him. It was 8:00 A.M. and he wanted to make love to a stranger, quietly, softly, without any possibility of interruption so that in the process he might figure out why she was blowing his mind.

So he concentrated on the salty taste of the bacon, the hot, sugar-sweet coffee, the fat buttermilk biscuits with his ex-girlfriend's prize-winning honey on top, the sides of the biscuits dripping Hiland brand butter, the brand Lillian favored so much she stocked the freezer with it in order to make sure she never ran out.

*I know, she'd said. What a cryptic answer.*

Miranda pushed her cup away, a common blue spongeware pattern set on a vintage Royal Copenhagen saucer, both pieces understated quality, like Brody's home, a well-loved, well-kept farmhouse.

Brody knew he'd disarmed her, not enough to stomp away from the table, but enough to quiet her hunger for food. "You didn't eat."

"I seldom eat breakfast," she said. "Lunch always. Dinner maybe."

So, he thought with relief, one cup of coffee was her normal routine. "No wonder you stay thin."

"Yes."

Her composure. He wanted badly to smash it to pieces, but he didn't know how. If she left right now, he wouldn't be able to stop her, wouldn't be able to shelter her within the safety of his home, the comfort of his arms. Never again would he know the warm feel of her lips against his own. Suddenly, never was a cold and lonely place to be. Too cold. Too lonely.

"Eventually," she said, "Lillian's biscuits and butter will fatten me up."

*Eventually*. Relief flooded through him, accelerated his heart rate. They both heard the housekeeper singsong the words *See you later alligators* as she bustled her way out of the front door, heard Lillian's Wrangler Jeep fire up, speed off. They were alone now, alone with secret wants, secret needs.

Miranda nodded her head. Her expression was as bland as ever, her eyes and manner revealing none of the sensual undertones she must be feeling. The air in the brightly lit kitchen was heavy with carnal appetites—the food, the drink, the intense intimacy of spending an entire night together, even though they were strangers.

"Yes," she said. "I know there won't be more biscuits with butter until Lillian comes home again."

"In three weeks."

"Yes. Three weeks."

All the air left his lungs in a rush. Some powerful, nameless emotion took possession of his heart. What was she saying? That she would be here long after Lillian returned?

It would be easy to get fat off these biscuits, but it would take some time. For once in his life, Brody Campbell, champion horse trainer, was held in suspense by a mysterious, beautiful woman, a woman with eyes that spoke to his soul.

She was confident without being arrogant. She was tormented by some demon that for him might remain unidentified. She was an artist, her ego expressed through the form and substance of her paintings.

Above all, she was honest, the trait in men and women he valued above all other traits, that and self-reliance. Perhaps this is what he found the most mysterious of all, the integrity she possessed, an honesty at odds with her rolling stone ways. In his experience, rolling stones were dependable for short stretches of time only.

He stood from the table, uncertain about the future, yet ready to claim it. The immediate future included Miranda. He didn't want to leave the kitchen, but he was committed to meeting potential clients at Remington Racetrack in Oklahoma City. God, he didn't want to go, he just didn't.

She, too, stood from the table. Instead of clearing her place setting, as he had done, she positioned herself in front of his face. She pulled him down, equal to her level. She peered into his eyes, breathed the air he exhaled. She pressed herself against him, intimately. She did something he would remember for all time, she kissed his warm, chocolate brown lips and said, "Thank you. For everything."

And then, she left him.

Duke appeared at the door. "Boss?"

No response.

"Boss!"

Brody was seriously distracted. Torn between

what he wanted to do, which was to pursue Miranda, and what he needed to do, which was to head to the racetrack, he finally said, "Yeah?"

"Genesis did it again."

"What?"

"I said, Genesis—" Duke broke off, his mouth twisted in disgust. "Never damn mind." The boss didn't seem to hear him; he was lost in space.

On his way to get the keys to his truck, Brody wondered if Miranda walked around barefoot all the time.

In her designated room, Miranda made her borrowed bed and put her shoes on. She itched to paint but knew she wasn't quite ready, soon, but not yet. She wanted to gain more of a feel of this place that welcomed her, of the man who so crudely expressed his wish to make love to her.

She wanted to be touched by him too, inside and out, but she didn't want to open herself to that kind of commitment; after all, he was a man she knew nothing about, a man who was generous and loving, but a stranger still.

Her gaze swept the restful ecru and white décor of the guest bedroom Lillian had chosen for her. The room was perfect. Nothing fancy, nothing too gender oriented, no satin, no lace. The only accent colors were hints of chocolate, of caramel, bay, bronze, and fawn.

A modern nomad, a wanderer, and a loner, she was revived by the peace she found here, in this room, this newfound sanctuary gifted to her by a man who believed in miracles. How else could he think he might save her, especially when the person she needed to be saved from was herself?

She wanted to destroy Leonard, literally kill him. All the walking she'd been doing since leaving Tulsa had been about putting distance between them, the kind of distance that wasn't easy to track down. He didn't expect her to do the impossible, which was to begin at the beginning.

In the beginning, she had a dream. In the dream, she had a home she adored, a man who believed in her as much as he believed in himself, and a calling to paint. In real life, she'd had access to those separate parts of the dream, only not at the same time. She was still dreaming.

She couldn't imagine a man like Brody betraying his wife by sleeping with another woman, no matter how badly he wanted an heir to whatever he intended to leave behind after his death.

She couldn't imagine him abandoning his marriage because his dreams of perfection were crushed by events beyond his control, such as finding out his wife couldn't bear him children by natural means.

Brody wasn't interested in status the way Leonard had been as a social climbing psychotherapist for the elite. Rather he was a man focused on quality and substance, on preservation of his heritage.

It was there, his commitment, in the proud way he surveyed his land, the way he cared for the people he employed—an elderly woman, once discarded by society because of her age, and an elderly ranch hand, who, Miranda guessed, was long on cowboy talent, short on people skills, a rambling man too old now to chase dreams.

Where Lillian had opened her arms to the wild woman Brody had brought home, Duke had kept his arms and his mouth shut. But his eyes, Miranda sighed at her first memory of them, his murky brown eyes had held hers in suspicion.

It was clear from the way his gaze bore through and dismissed her that he distrusted her presence on Campbell land, an unescorted woman who refused to declare her past or her intentions for the future.

She was a rolling stone. Duke knew all about rolling stones because he was a drifter himself. Drifters were the kind of people who lived without commitment to any particular property, place, or person. Not having emotional attachments made it easy to pick up and go whenever the mood struck.

But what about Brody? she wondered. What about a man who exposed his back to an alien woman, a woman extrinsic to the landscape he treasured, a woman he left alone in his house? Was he truly that trusting? Or did he practice the philosophy she lived—what is, is, and what hasn't happened shouldn't be worried about until it did?

Young, single, and hard-working, he could approach any woman he wanted. Handsome, land rich, and flexible in his thinking, he'd be skilled at managing the details in life; so why would he confess to her, a troubled woman, his desire to make love?

Did he feel the way she did? As if his breath stirred the fine hairs on her body so that the skin beneath felt caressed? Did his pulse quicken when she spoke, as hers did when she felt the rumble of his voice in the base of her stomach? Did he like the round shape of her chin, as she admired the square set of his?

Having held her snug between his thighs atop Genesis, did he imagine now the feel of her bare skin to the point that he spoke his desire out loud? Perhaps, unlike her, he had nothing to hide, even from a visitor in his home.

When she was sure he'd left the house, Miranda familiarized herself with the property, her way of centering herself. Never having been in a barn for horses, she made this area her first destination.

The building was one and a half stories tall, a large rectangle colored a rich redwood, its doors white, its trim and roof a deep blue. Four flat rectangles of white windows broke the blue expanse of the roof. The barn matched the house and other outbuildings. She left her place on the path to enter.

The barn was a six-stall structure, reinforced with galvanized steel. All the walls were white, as were the numerous lighting fixtures. The stalls were littered with cedar shavings, which she assumed served the double purpose of odor control and bedding for the horses, which were all outside.

There was a work room filled with cabinets and hooks, a large triple sink, long counters, and a heavy steel table. There were saddles and a myriad other horse-related supplies, from leg wraps to shampoos and conditioners, all within easy reach, all tidy and clean in appearance. Stairs led to the half story loft, and at the top of the stairs stood Duke.

"Ain't nothing for you here," he said. He spoke slow, his voice raspy, like a long kitchen match striking brick. His wide brimmed hat was hard and grubby white. His clothes were heavy blue denim, the pants matching the jacket, his shirt red and charcoal checkered, his boots so banged up and worn out they looked as old and kick-butt mean as he did. He spit a long stream of chewing tobacco into the cedar shavings on the floor, his eyes dead center with hers.

Slightly unnerved that he'd been studying her without her being aware of it, and doing it with such open hostility, Miranda conjured an image of Leonard. The image helped her find the courage to fight Duke.

It was the same gumption that helped her travel across the state of Oklahoma with only her wit and her talent to guide her. Duke Ransaw could jump off the nearest bridge for all she cared.

She used her eyes and tone to tell him so. "I don't like you either, but that's not the point of my being here—to be liked that is."

Duke's features were as closed and hard as a convict stuck on an Alabama chain gang. At that moment, his face was intense, brutal, withering, with no glimpse of the true inner workings of his mind.

"No respectable woman would live as you do." He spat again, into the shavings, this time a full foot closer to Miranda's feet.

"Who and what I am is none of your business," she said, her glance more a dismissal than an invitation to talk. He might have been a lowly stable boy and she a pampered princess for all the scorn she poured into her voice. So what if she didn't live here for real? She wasn't hurting anybody. Besides, she'd been asked to stay.

Duke's durable, weathered skin tightened across his face. He didn't bother to put a lid on his contempt. "Brody Campbell is my business."

"He doesn't have a problem," she said, as if the watcher at the top of the stairs was trespassing on her turf. In this case, her turf was her privacy. She threw just enough guts into her attitude to let him know she didn't have any chicken in her. Only cowards were chickens. "Lillian doesn't have a problem, either."

The old man worked his chew a full two beats. He wasn't to be distracted with thoughts of Lillian, who, before she left for Guthrie, had told him to mind his own business, not Brody's.

Duke said, "Brody trusts too easy."

"Brody is the boss."

Duke descended four quick steps before he checked himself. He wanted to shake the little conniver, wanted to drive her all the way to Kingfisher County and leave her there in the dust. "Lillian is checking with the Logan County Sheriff to see if they know anything bad about you."

If he thought to scare her into flight, scare her into admitting some serious crime of some sort, then he was thoroughly disappointed when all she did was look the same way she'd look at a rodent.

"You stay out of my way," she said, "I'll stay out of yours."

She sauntered out of the barn, her facial muscles

totally in control, her steps even, her pulse at its normal rate. Perhaps this is the reason he trailed after her, to strike a blow to her demeanor, to pressure her into admitting that her reasons for being on Campbell land were self-serving, maybe even dangerously corrupt in some way.

Miranda didn't care what he did, because she didn't care about the wandering woman she'd become since abandoning her marriage to Leonard. All she cared about was her three-dimensional imagery, work that served as her personal, prolific mark in the modern African American art world.

This body of work was her legacy, a gift of her creative nature expressed time and time again. This was the visible, tragic piece of her being that was reflected now and then in her eyes. Painting was the fuel she lived on, the use of food, clothing, and shelter the necessary evils of the human flesh. No, she wasn't afraid of Duke anymore than she was afraid of Leonard—or a wild coyote.

Miranda ambled her physically fit body over the peaceful terrain as if Brody's tobacco chewing right-hand man didn't exist. She stopped now and then to search the property with her eyes, several scrubby miles of it, her gaze lingering briefly on the storage buildings within her sight, the abandoned outhouse, the potting shed, empty now of everything but assorted farm tools, buckets, car parts, and just plain junk.

It was the round pen that settled her eye. Inside its circular wood structure stood a mother with her young colt, gorgeous, both of them creamy-colored quarter horses.

Without formal thought, Miranda's right hand did more than itch to paint, it moved in the air of its own volition, sketched the mother and child, then reached for a brush that wasn't there, thus breaking the spell she'd been under.

Behind her, Duke stopped dogging her every slow step. He spit on the ground. "Crazy bitch."

Miranda felt crazy too, crazy enough to feel as if she'd come home, but she couldn't share these thoughts with the barely law-abiding citizen stalking behind her. She couldn't tell this to anyone, not her, a woman who pretended as if the day before hadn't existed, who didn't believe in tomorrow, who had no stake in today.

She couldn't tell him, this seasoned wanderer, that she was tired of being alone, tired of trying to forget a past she could neither escape nor accept. Leonard probably had missing persons bulletins posted about her, not because he loved her, not because he worried about her, or even missed her, but because he couldn't get the divorce he wanted, as fast as he wanted it.

He couldn't gain the closure he required in order to make his new family with Tessa and Leonard Junior, a legitimate legal unit. This petty betrayal on her part was a finely felt and bittersweet revenge.

*Ah yes*, Miranda mused, *Leonard Junior*. Her petty betrayal felt damned good.

She pivoted so sharply she rammed into Duke, who looked like a wolf with his fangs out. It was clear he despised her presence in his territory. Very probably she should be afraid of him, but how could she be afraid when rogue coyotes hadn't made her run for her life?

His counterpart, the kind and giving Lillian, might be, at this very moment, in the Logan County Sheriff's office, accessing information about her. What could she do about Duke? About Lillian? Nothing.

Was this why Brody was so relaxed? Did he know that Duke, in his extreme possessiveness, would dog her as he did today, dog her until she felt stalked and intimidated into either confessing her sins or taking the high road once again? Did he know that Lillian wasn't as accepting as she'd first appeared?

Of course he knew.

He didn't impress her as a man who left many stones unturned. Yes, he'd listen to their reports about her past and her present. He'd use their input to reassess and enforce his own system for dealing with her. Wise men always listened.

Apparently, Brody Campbell listened to his heart. Why else would he grant her sanctuary in this Eden he called home? Eden in the form of a delightful place to live, an environment that fed the five senses of the human world, their world. For the artist in Miranda, this place was a haven, a solace and refuge. She could breathe here.

Thank God for Brody. His eyes were not the hard, suspicious eyes of Duke, his voice was not the polite window dressing used by Lillian, both people, Miranda suspected, simply protective of their hero, her hero, and for this, she couldn't fault them. Brody's heart was a valuable thing in this windy, clay-packed land, Campbell land.

In truth, she was tired of heading nowhere special, tired of wearing the same clothes, the same shoes. She missed getting her hair done by a professional, missed lazy bubble baths with jazz playing in the background. She missed having a studio, something she hadn't realized until she saw the potting shed.

If she took the frayed curtains off its windows, the shed would be filled with light. She could stuff planters with dangling geranium in blue, some tiny leafed ivy. If she . . . only belonged to this place, this beautiful land of deep ponds and ravines and wild animals that sang in the night.

If only . . .

She could store her paints in a place like this shed. There would be solitude all around her, horses in the distance, horses . . . Her gaze was caught by the return of Brody, his head covered in a vented work hat as hard and grubby as Duke's hat. His jeans were loosened up now and comfy, his boots embedded with red Oklahoma dirt.

But it was his aura that licked the wounds on her soul. His aura exuded confidence, his demeanor touched with the kind of southern charm that was inbred and cultivated one generation after another. His hands—yes, she found a man's hands very attractive indeed—guided two unbridled horses down a well-traveled path to the barn.

Gently, through his will and soft touch alone, he showed the horses he loved them, loved the way they moved, the way they existed, and they followed him, not blindly, but in faith that upon their destination, food, water, and a place to rest awaited them. Miranda's fingers sketched the air, brush-stroked the first imaginary color of her design.

Behind her, Duke cleared his throat. "Lady," he said, "if you hurt him, I swear on my mama's grave I'll make you sorry you was ever born."

She faced him then, her eyes so broken his breath snagged in his throat. He choked on his own spit so that he gagged a little and coughed a lot. She left him there, coughing until he regained his composure, until his fists unclenched them-selves, until he wondered who and what had destroyed her will to survive.

Now he knew why Brody had taken her in, why Lillian had told him she would check with the au-thorities, all the while doubting anything negative would come of it, not caring if it did.

Staring at the foundling's back, Duke felt some-thing he hadn't felt in so long the feeling was rusty—that feeling was shame. He wondered, like Lillian and Brody, what he could do to help this woman whose mind wasn't screwed too tight.

From a barn window, Brody watched her stride purposefully to the house. He wondered what she planned to do next. Would she grab the paints she so obviously craved, or would she sit on the side of her borrowed bed, pondering the future?

He'd bet Genesis she was searching for the perfect spot to lay the first stroke of the imaginary brush she held in her hand. What disturbed Brody most was Duke, his open antagonism, his spitting, his stalking, the verbal confrontation, and yet he understood his friend's intentions as deeply as he recognized the pain scored into Miranda's black eyes.

Someone had wrecked the road to her soul. Maybe, just maybe, painting was the last way she knew to reconnect her mind to her body and whatever spirit she had left to find. When Brody next spied her, she was stepping off the porch, knapsack strung from one loop on one small shoulder.

Her face bordered on desperation as she sought release from the need to keep herself tightly wound and meticulously maintained. She had to paint, had to paint now, he could tell, tell it in the way she was frantic to find a place to land her feet, to plant her box of paints, to give birth to the vision only she could see.

Brody's fascination shifted from the mentally unbalanced woman who lived in his home to the cantankerous ranch hand he trusted with his life.

Duke entered the barn, then hooked a stool from against a wall with his Wolverine brand work boot. "How'd you know?"

"That she needed protection?"

Duke simply nodded his head.

"Same way you did."

"Those eyes."

"Yeah," Brody said. "Those eyes."

"Think Lillian will find anything on her?"

Brody stared through the wide, dusty barn windows as if he might see Miranda again. But he couldn't see her, and so he pictured her as he'd spied her last, hauntingly beautiful, emotionally disturbed, tragically alone, in a hurry to create something new for the planet.

When he spoke, it was a certainty he felt in his bones. "Nothing so wrong it can't be fixed fairly easy. Don't think she's built that way, living with the law after her neck. I just don't see it that way."

The spitting man nodded once in assent. Still, there was something wrong with Miranda, something he didn't completely trust. "Lillian must have come to the same conclusion we did about the girl."

Brody laughed, the sound full of affection. "Yeah," he said. "She did."

Duke shot him a glance that left no room for secrets, no room at all. "What did it for you? Finding her in the dirt like that?"

Brody searched his mind for the words that would describe what he felt for Miranda, but he couldn't because he wasn't sure himself. He just knew he couldn't let her go, not now, when she desperately needed—what? To be needed herself? To be treated as if she mattered?

"It was her art," he said at length.

"On your brother's walls."

"Yeah."

When the silence shifted into something moody and brooding, Duke stood. He shoved the stool back against the wall. "Tell me."

"When I first saw her work, I had the impression of a kitten, lost and frightened, burrowing itself into a nest of leaves, hidden in the hollow of something long dead and forgotten."

"A kitten?"

Brody didn't miss the subtle sarcasm. He sounded like a love struck fool and he knew it, but so what, his feelings were real. "A kitten."

Duke's tone was set on cool, his shuttered eyes

giving no hint to whatever he felt inside. "You think that's what she is?"

"No. She wouldn't have survived on the road in the top shape she's in if she wasn't confident. It was the . . . essence of a small-vulnerable-creature-after-safety kind of thing I had in mind. I can't explain it any better."

Duke couldn't or wouldn't let it go. "You mean, what? The feeling of it?"

At the risk of sounding even more silly and poetic in front of his friend, Brody exposed a little more of himself. He could do this with Duke, a man whose opinion he valued, however salty it might be.

Having lived his entire life in the rural southwest, Brody understood and accepted the general common sense of his elders, especially loyal, hardworking men such as Duke. Clearly, Duke wanted to call him three shades of fool; the fact he didn't voice that opinion was sincerely appreciated.

So Brody answered his question. "Exactly," he said. "It's like trying to describe the color and shape of a single drop of rain in such a way as to be able to imagine the way it would taste."

Duke coughed, spit, and walked out.

Brody resisted the urge to search for Miranda, knowing it was he who was lost, she who was found. He needed to think and he couldn't think straight with a sorceress in sight.

Without a doubt, she'd worked some kind of magic spell on him, a spell that kept him tempted, kept him curious, kept him wanting to do what Duke had done, which was follow her around as if he had nothing better to do with his time, which was far from the truth on a working ranch that housed twenty or more horses at a time.

Miranda had seen him watching her, watching her the way he'd watched the horses he'd led to the barn. She saw something there, in his eyes, the desire to deal with her the way he dealt with his equine charges, with touch, intuition, and the kind of passion that only a true animal lover can bring to the table.

The question was, would she let him do it, touch her? Would she let him smooth his dry, rough hands gently over the curves of her body, his fingers exerting pressure here and there, just enough pressure to suggest control, but never enough pressure to intimidate? Would she? Would she let him do that? Want and need were two different things. She wanted him, yes, but she didn't need him. Need implied obligation. She walked away from obligation when she left Tulsa.

Want versus need.

Brody was drop-dead gorgeous, the kind of handsome that dominated western-styled romance novels, smack down to the tough, chiseled look of absolute maleness, of intense physicality, of ingrained nobility, the kind of nobility that never left a damsel in distress. Brody was the style of man with a heart huge enough to adore a cynical old man and a nosey old woman.

His was the kind of robust male power that wasn't limited to mere machismo, but rather, his power was enhanced by the way he reveled in his maleness. It was there in the myth-driven image of a man and his horse, not just any horse, but a stallion. In this case, a horse as huge and heavily muscled, as virile as the man who rode him with the kind of confidence that came from dealing with horses from the cradle.

Only this wasn't a tale about a man being conquered by a woman. Rather it was a tale about a man trying to conquer a woman who happened to be a rebel without a cause. Causes were all about good intentions. She had no good intentions.

She once had a cause, her art, but she was no longer living for that cause. Her art had become a matter of economics, a tool for survival. She was living for revenge. Revenge was all about punishment.

The person she wanted to punish was Leonard. She was a rebel all right, but she had no illusions about the kind of woman she'd become. A fallen woman. A woman bent on destruction.

If she wanted anything beyond revenge it was absolution from life, not the kind of remission from sin and penalties granted by religious figures, but absolution free from the restrictions of being in a certain place at a certain time for any particular reason. Her existence was perfect in that she survived on the most basic levels. It was a liberating process. Once liberated she had no wish to be confined again.

If Brody had been a mountain man, pitting himself against the elements to forge himself a new self, maybe then he'd understand her wish to be alone. If he'd been a philosopher, like Epictetus, he might understand that in her mind, she was free.

But he was Brody, a man so full of life and love he couldn't stand to see someone live without the comfort of tradition, the solace of friendship. For him, to live her way was to live with no sun.

If only he knew how on target he was. Leonard had been her sun. She had orbited around him, absorbed his heat, thrived on it, and now she was so cold she didn't know how to go about feeling warm again.

Son, no heir.

Sun, no life.

In the months since leaving Leonard, she'd been as aimless as paper blowing in the wind. If someone picked the paper up, it could be written on, thus made useful again, dirty but useful; but as long as the paper remained in motion, it was almost worthless.

This described Miranda, useful when she worked, useless when she didn't work because when she wasn't working, she produced no effect on her environment. Only when she stopped her wandering, when she stopped long enough to paint, did she carve a notch in the tree of life. If it wasn't for her art, she would leave the world without a legacy.

Shame and anger had driven her away from Tulsa. She knew her parents and extended family worried about her. Even though they'd be glad to have her back, they'd make her sorry she'd returned to them once again.

After the sweetness of knowing she was safe had worn smooth, anger would set in, recrimination. She'd embarrassed them. All that drama belonged to yesterday, and for Miranda, yesterday didn't count. She lived in the moment. The moment was now.

It was spite that spurred her onward. She didn't want to give Leonard a divorce. She didn't care if his natural heir had a properly married mother and father, but she did care about her studio; she did, but, like a child, that too was a casualty of her marital war.

Miranda drew a bracing breath. Here she was, living in today. Today she was in the small setting of a rural farm on the central plains of Oklahoma. By chance or by religious design, she'd found work in the homes of brothers. The first commission had paved the way for Brody's trust, simply because he trusted his own brother's judgment.

But it was Brody who stimulated her thought process, Brody who made her pulse warp speed, made heat burn her face and throat and chest when he drew near. If it was true, what she sensed, that he was planning to catapult her into living a full life again, she was finding his efforts difficult to resist. It was hard to resist him because he presented a package deal she found attractive.

She found his property attractive. Having spent so much time on the road, the variety of wildlife that thrived undisturbed by man appealed to her. Miranda could flex in a place like this, a place that wasn't saturated with rushing people and fast cars and other types of congestion.

In Brody, she'd found sanctuary, immunity from questions about her past, refuge against physical terrors, hope in the form of desire and expectation—the desire to paint, the expectation of turning bare areas around the Campbell homestead into works of art. Inside her was this delicious shift from the hopeless throes of revenge to the hopeful quest of being a rounded person again.

She knew what he was doing, that he was easing up on her the way he eased up on his horses, finessing the distance between them with compassion, the first element of trust. He wasn't forcing her in place with threats or intimidation, but like an athlete in a western calf-roping event, he used a well-placed rope to trap and guide her. Yes, she was afraid of falling, falling back into humanity, that place that hurt so much.

Miranda couldn't touch Brody's rope with her hands, but with her mind, she sensed its presence, there in the boundaries of his property, beautiful acres and acres of it in every direction she turned.

He coaxed her into testing the waters of life by exposing her to bare walls in need of paint, not the traditional slap of one-coat exterior paint, but the stroke of artistry that drove her to do as she did right now, kneel at the post marking the left entrance of the long drive to the main house.

Brush in hand, she drew horses leaving the gate, Genesis in the lead, his head angled in the direction of the single whistle drawing him back to the family fold, his renegade equine friends in tow.

Yes, Brody Campbell was a dangerous man, dangerous like a thief.

# Five

Carmen Oliver was tall, dark, and dangerously close to losing her cool over Brody. He was the only man she'd ever loved. She loved him more than she loved the hair growing thick to the middle of her back.

When she thought good and hard about it, she one day realized that she loved him more than the taste of chocolate, of wild, sweet berries straight off the summer vine. Her passion for him was unfortunate. He didn't love her back.

She aimed her frustration at Miranda, who looked as if she didn't have a care in the world. "How dare you vandalize this place?"

"Find Brody. He'll tell you what you need to know."

It had been two weeks, and already Miranda had painted the posts flanking the entrance to Brody's drive, the steps to the front and back doors of his house, the frames along the barn windows, the south wall of Lillian's bedroom.

She'd paint all day and half the night. She'd rise early, have breakfast with Brody, never once touching, but wanting to touch him, never once asking if he still wanted to make love to her. She knew in her heart that he did and was thankful he didn't pursue the subject. Sex would further complicate an already complicated relationship.

Now there was this Carmen chick to deal with whether she wanted to deal with her or not, which she didn't. She assessed her opponent. The new woman had skin the color of autumn maple leaves, eyes the color of fresh-toasted almonds. She was lean, strong as packing cord, and, at the moment, mad as a red wasp.

The women were in front of the round pen, Miranda smudged with paint, Carmen astride Destiny, a gelding thoroughbred as black as Genesis, as strong as Genesis, but more sleek, more long legged, and much more classy.

Alerted by Duke, Brody had arrived on the scene ready to shove the women apart if they got into it. On any given day, neither one of them took any guff. He expected a fight.

He looked at Carmen in a way he hadn't looked at her since they'd broken up three months before—with more than a cursory glance. She had on a khaki-colored Resistol hat with a matching scarf wrapped around her neck, a cream Henley sweater tucked inside faded Cruel Girl jeans.

She wore Lisa Sorrell custom boots, cognac colored and kangaroo skinned, on feet that knew how to kick ass when necessary. She was a tough woman to love. She had to have her own way most of the time or she wasn't happy.

His voice was heavy. "What do you want, Carmen?"

She didn't say, *you*, but it was there in her eyes when she took her fill of him. "Answers."

Brody wished she'd move on, as he had. She lived in the past. Analyzed it. Picked at it. Wouldn't let it go. In her own way, she was as possessive of him as Duke was. "Shoot."

"I want to," she said. "Shoot her that is."

"You don't even know her."

"I know she doesn't belong."

"Neither do you."

Clearly, she was hurt. "Bastard."

He shrugged. "Sometimes."

Miranda threw her paints into the box Brody had given to her for that purpose. He said it was a box he no longer had need for; however, she could tell it was quite new, no scratches, no scuffs, with a just-off-the-shelf scent. It had been sitting beside her bedroom door one morning during her first week in residence.

"'Scuse me, folks," she said. "Three's a crowd."

Neither Carmen nor Brody tried to stop her from leaving. They were glaring at each other so hard she could have been talking to herself. They didn't spare a glance in her direction as she passed them by.

Their horses weren't all that comfortable, and she didn't want to be around if they started acting up. She didn't fight in other people's battles or try to understand them. She had enough of her own problems to deal with.

"You can't be serious, Brody," Carmen said. "She's a tramp for God's sake."

"Watch it."

"She's got paint under her nails. On her face. She's a weirdo I'm telling you. Rumor has it she wears the same clothes every day."

"She's an artist."

Disgusted, Carmen's top lip curled. "Artist my foot. She's not even moody or temperamental. She acts like she's from some other world or something. I mean, she's so self-absorbed."

Brody couldn't believe she had the nerve to chastise him about the way he conducted his private business. "We broke her concentration."

Carmen didn't miss the flash of anger in his eyes. "You act like we're the trespassers here."

Brody was careful to keep his voice even. He was tired of explaining himself. He did it this time out of friendship and kindness. Worn friendship. Thin kindness. "She's welcome. Besides, she's not your problem."

"So. You admit there's a problem."

"What are you doing here, Carmen?"

"News travels fast, Brody. You know that. I'm spying, OK? I mean, what else do you think I'd be doing?"

In truth, he was surprised it had taken her two weeks to make a visit. "How about being a Good Samaritan? How about being a friend to her?"

She looked at him as if he were crazy. "I don't do tea parties."

"That's not what I'm talking about."

"I don't like her."

He shook his head. "Try getting to know her first."

"Like you did?"

"Those were different circumstances."

Carmen shrugged. "Not really. I found her alone, where she didn't belong. You found her alone, where she didn't belong. Same difference."

"Go home."

She thought for a minute. "I'll go home, but I'll be back."

"Why?"

"To be a friend. I'm gonna make ya'll dinner."

At dinner, Carmen made a point of proving to Miranda she knew where every spoon, knife, fork, and ladle belonged. She went straight to the oils, the seasonings, the vegetables as she fried the fish she'd trapped that afternoon.

Duke had announced he was going to the Blue Belle Saloon in Guthrie and would miss dinner. Brody had laughed, stating that Duke was a coward, to which Duke had said, "Got that right."

In the kitchen, Miranda took her usual seat, which happened to be Carmen's usual seat. She draped a cloth napkin over her lap.

Carmen was outdone. "That's my chair."

Miranda smiled, only she didn't show her teeth.

"I said, that's my chair."

Miranda helped herself to iced tea.

"How dare you ignore me?"

Miranda didn't look at her. "I dare a lot of things."

Carmen accepted the chair Brody pulled out for her, at the head of the table, opposite Miranda. He sat in between them, in case it was necessary for him to referee, which he expected he might have to do before this meal was done.

"Ladies," he said, "let's find something neutral to talk about."

Miranda savored the sliced squash, which had

been smothered in onions and cheddar cheese. "This is wonderful."

Carmen was caught between pleasure at the compliment and the need to get a dig in. "Grew the squash and onions myself."

"Tastes like it."

Carmen put her fork down. "What kind of comment is that?"

"The food is fresh," Miranda explained. "Relax."

Brody looked as if he wanted to be anywhere but at a table that was quickly becoming a battlefield. He went after their attention. "Ladies?"

The ladies ignored him.

Carmen eyed Miranda's plate. "You haven't any fish on your plate, so how can you say the food is wonderful when you haven't tried all the food?"

Brody thought it was a good time to talk about the weather. "Ladies?"

"I haven't tried all the food because I don't care for catfish."

"It's farm fed," Carmen said. "The fish get to swim, so they aren't musty smelling or tasting or anything."

"No," Miranda said, "but, thank you."

Brody snagged another fish from the serving plate.

Carmen glared at him. "Stop it."

Miranda laughed, the sound soft and full of mockery. "Are you always this controlling? Do this. Do that. Stop this. Stop that."

Carmen's upper body swelled with indignation. "How dare you criticize me? This isn't your house. He's not your man."

Miranda thought about how she and Brody danced along the edges of sex every time they shared a meal at this very table. Maybe that was the energy pushing Carmen's jealousy into overdrive. Maybe she sensed a romance developing between them. Only Miranda didn't want a romance. She wanted to paint, nothing more, nothing less. She'd already tackled Duke and Lillian. Carmen didn't fit with the program.

"This isn't your house, either," she said. "Get over it."

Carmen made a rake of her fingers. She swung her arm across the table with enough force to create wind in the still kitchen air.

Brody caught her wrist before contact. "Time to go."

She snatched her wrist from his grasp. "You defend this, this tramp, and then tell me to get outta here?"

Brody's face was grim. "Miranda is able to defend herself."

"So, why are you kicking me outta the house?"

"Because I can't stand rudeness, especially at the dinner table and especially when the rudeness is done out of spite."

"I made this meal."

"You barged in here to claim a territory that's no longer yours, Carmen. We're finished, remember?"

"We'll never be finished."

Miranda scraped her chair back from the table. "'Scuse me."

"Don't," Brody said, staying her physically by encircling her wrist. He did it gently, his voice a caress.

Carmen threw her napkin on the table. She stomped a kangaroo boot on the floor hard enough to shake the chairs. She sucked in a deep breath. She leaned toward Miranda. "You don't belong here."

She left out the word bitch, but the word was there anyway. She turned to Brody. "I grew up here. With you."

"Not in this house you didn't. We've been friends all our lives, Carmen. It was a mistake to go for more than that."

"We were great together," she said. "We made love. You wouldn't have done that if you didn't care."

Brody ran an open palm over his face as if to ask, *How did we get to this place, this particular conversation?* "You're one of my oldest friends. We share a past no one can take away from us, but you know as well as I do that no matter how hard we tried, the sparks were never real."

Carmen carried on as if they didn't have an audience of one. "I didn't chase you, Brody Campbell."

Miranda spoke into the silence. "You're so beautiful. You can have any man you want, why force—"

Carmen slammed a fist against the table. "I've never in my life forced a man to do anything he didn't want to do."

"Really?" Miranda said. "You're forcing this issue right here. You forced your will and way into this kitchen to prove a point to a woman you don't even know, all out of some misguided sense of jealousy. I'm an artist. If you look around, you'll see my work all over the property. I sleep in the guest room. I'm no threat to you."

Carmen starting clearing the table. Her movements were mechanical, her face immobile as a rock.

Brody didn't trust her. He angled his body slightly so that in one step or less, he'd be in front of Miranda in order to protect her.

The air was tense and thick, ripe with suppressed anger. Miranda allowed it to wash over and around her, never through her, something she could do because, unlike them, her emotions were not engaged. She could afford to be objective.

She said, "Let's talk this out."

They looked at her as if she had horns where her ears should be.

"Really," she said, "come on." She moved to sit closer to Carmen, so that she now sat across from Brody.

Carmen eyeballed him. "I can't believe you're letting her call the shots."

"We all know how you feel, Carmen. No one is making you stay."

She looked hurt. "I only want what's mine."

"I don't belong to you," he said quietly. "Never did." To Miranda, he said, "Floor is yours."

"First of all, I'm here because I want to be."

Carmen snorted. "You're here because Brody found you face down in the dirt. You were like a dog all laid out to die."

Brody exploded. "Carmen!"

Miranda patted him on the arm. "Big girls handle their own business. You handle yours. I'll handle mine."

Carmen licked her lips. "Yeah, Brody. Be quiet."

He wanted to evict them both. He crossed his arms. "Five minutes, ladies. Show'll be over after that."

Carmen's eyes glittered. "You think so?"

"I know so."

The ladies could tell he meant what he said, too.

Miranda went first. "I was depressed when Brody found me."

"So, it's true then," Carmen said. "You wanted to die."

"Yes."

"Why?"

"Why not?"

Carmen was truly shocked. "Everyone wants to live, Miranda."

"I was tired of struggling to live the way I want to live."

Carmen peered into her face. "How is that?"

Miranda held on to her defenses. "Let's deal in today only."

Brody had learned to respect her privacy. He backed her up before Carmen could argue. "Today it is, then."

While Carmen struggled for composure, he considered how well everyone had been getting along until she showed up. He'd been doing his own thing with his horses. Miranda had been doing her thing with her painting.

Duke had been doing what he always did, which was to oversee the property and the people who lived there. Maybe that was Carmen's problem, life with Miranda had been going too well. Her invasion was a test of sorts.

In gratitude, Miranda tried to meet Brody half way. She tried to explain things to Carmen. "Today, all I wanted to do was paint."

Carmen opted for civility as well. She was worried Brody would kick her out of the house if she didn't behave. "That's when I came along."

"Yes. You and your will. Your opinions. Your wants. You forced yourself into my space with your criticism. My world. I'm tired of messing around with people like you. I just want to be left alone. Period."

Carmen was cold and derisive. "I don't know why Brody gives you the time of day except that he pities you."

Miranda didn't care what Carmen thought about her. She only cared about the current program, the status quo until she got ready to pack her bags. She wasn't ready to do that yet. "Brody is man enough to let me be the woman I am."

Carmen snorted. "You've got balls, Miss Thing. I'll give you that much."

Miranda wanted to punch Carmen's lights out. "So sayeth the woman scorned."

Carmen's sneer was vicious. "I can't believe you."

"I can't believe you, either. You've got enough money to ride your own racehorse. You hunt and cook your own food. You wear thousand-dollar custom-made boots. You're gorgeous. Well-spoken. But then you turn around and chase a man who only wants to be your friend. I may be crazy, but I know when to cut my losses."

Carmen was speechless.

So was Brody.

Miranda wasn't finished. "You think I'm a tramp. It's true. I am. Tramps travel with no destination."

"Aimlessly you mean."

Miranda smiled that no-teeth smile again. "Aimless suggests no purpose. I'm actually confining my travels to the state of Oklahoma."

"Your travels?"

"Yes, Carmen, my travels. I've seen more of Oklahoma than you've probably seen in your lifetime. I'm not talking about the inside of hotel rooms, restaurants, and equestrian sports arenas like the Lazy E here in Guthrie. I'm talking about the land, the people, the smells, the emotion."

Brody was mesmerized. "You're like Zora Neale Hurston, the Harlem Renaissance writer who traveled through small southern towns recording black folklore."

Miranda, for the first time since leaving her husband, felt emotion, raw, red emotion. This man, this cowboy, saw the world beneath her skin. He was beginning to understand her.

Carmen was outraged. "Don't tell me you admire her?"

"I do."

"Why?" Carmen wailed.

Brody ignored her and spoke to Miranda instead. "I read once that Alice Walker put a headstone on Hurston's unmarked grave."

Miranda eyed him funny. "So?"

"Hurston was an anthropologist. Because of her, a major southern heritage was salvaged. She saved sermons, work songs, hoodoo rituals, games, and stories in general. She recorded the way rural black people lived, but when she died, it was in poverty. She became a success largely after her death."

Both women were surprised by his knowledge.

His smile was rueful. "My mother is really into folklore. She knows all sorts of stories about black life in the south. She's from the Mississippi delta region. She and my father met at Langston University."

Miranda nodded. "The black college about twenty miles from here."

"Yeah. You really did your homework before heading this way."

Carmen was mad as hell. "Would you just stop it, Brody? I mean, she doesn't even have a car and you're talking about 'heading this way.' Please. She's a vagrant for crying out loud. A loose woman or something."

Miranda acted as if Carmen's outburst never happened. She said to Brody, "I always do my homework."

"Really?" Carmen said. "What does it matter about this Zora Neale Hurston or Alice Walker or Miranda Evans?"

It surprised Brody when Miranda answered the question that had been directed to him, but it was with a question of her own. "Have you ever wondered where human civilization would be without artists to record it?"

"She's right," Brody said. "The drawings of cavemen on the walls of their homes, photographers capturing the last great fighters of the Indian Wars. . . ."

Miranda's smile was soft and genuine. At last,

someone had a true inkling of what really fired her up. "Men like Geronimo."

"Yeah." He smiled in return. "Like Geronimo."

Carmen was disgusted. "I'm gonna go home."

Neither Brody nor Miranda said a word. They were still connected by the thread of fresh discovery, the unique humanity that defined their true natures and sense of selves.

Carmen cleared her throat. "I said," she paused for emphasis, "I'm going home."

Miranda shifted her gaze from Brody to Carmen, so that at last, Carmen understood why Brody, a man who gained the trust of wild and injured things, would be attracted to Miranda: Miranda had been hurt badly by somebody somewhere, and the pain was so deep it still showed. Her eyes were blacker than night, older than justice. She had the kind of strength that didn't have a bottom to it, the kind of will that knew how to shift and bend with the idiosyncrasies of life.

Carmen was jealous.

In the wake of her departure, Brody said, "If I were a drinking man, I'd want a shot of something about now."

Miranda laughed. The musical sound of it left him ruined for the sound of any other woman's laughter. He recognized, in this laugh, that she was far from helpless; she was alone, yes, but not helpless. She was entirely self-contained. She didn't need him, but she wanted him.

Her want was there in the way she angled her body toward him, not openly flirtatious or preening, but with all her femininity and intelligence

aimed directly at him. He was polarized, magne-
tized, and yes, hypnotized.

A woman like Miranda offered a man his freedom, not in the sense that he could chase other
women, or stay out all night without being asked
why. But rather she offered a man the chance
to be his own man, someone enhanced and en-
riched because she was his significant other. A
man could relax around a self-contained woman
like her.

He could sit down after a long day of work, put
his feet on the table without her cramming a list of
honey-do's down his throat. He could do those
things because she'd lived her day to its maximum,
as he had.

She'd be putting her feet on the table to vegetate
after dinner, just like him. She knew when to talk,
when to listen, when to simply be quiet. Carmen
kept her foot on the pedal and the pedal had been
his neck.

As dusk turned to night, and the only light in the
room shone down from the chandelier above their
heads, he said, "Is that why you do it?"

"Do what?"

"Paint your soul on the walls of the places you've
been?"

"My soul?" She looked shocked.

He could think of no better way to describe his
interpretation of her work. He'd studied it from
every angle. "Yeah. Your soul."

His depth of character touched something deep
in her. He moved her physically, emotionally. The
buried parts of her were beginning to reveal them-

selves to the light, his light. This man took her at face value, and she was thankful for this approach.

She felt a fraud though, knowing she had a husband who wanted to know if she was dead or alive. "I try to record what I feel about what I see, the small pleasures in life that go unnoticed if someone doesn't stop to jot them down."

"Someone like you."

"Yes. Someone . . . like me."

For Miranda, the spell shared between them was broken, and so she sat there, at a table cluttered with cold food, the atmosphere tainted by the harsh words of Carmen, silent now, because she was reminded of the music behind her own madness.

She was mad wasn't she? Crazy to leave her art studio, with its three-dimensional designs depicting the poverty and wealth of pioneer black Oklahomans. She recalled how her mission had started, with her discovery of the Tulsa riots in 1921, the remnants of it, and then the recording of them.

Leonard had never understood this, her passion for reporting the isms and injustices, the era-bound pleasures of the people she researched, the places and things that influenced her own worldviews. Brody understood her muse, her art, but he wouldn't understand her leaving her husband.

Rapt, he watched the transition in her demeanor. A stone wall had gone up. A moat had been constructed. He wanted to recapture those slender, fleeting few moments after his ex-girlfriend's departure. He said, "I admire you."

She knew that he did too, admire her, because it was there in the slow groove of his eyes, this man whose mother had filled his child-mind with stories of heroes and legends.

Men became legends because of their clear sense of the just and the right. Brody was this kind of hero, the kind who never gave into the odds. If he'd given up on her that very first day, she'd never know that a horse could break his friends out of jail for the hell of it. She'd never know a man who whispered his way into the hearts of horses. She'd never know the peace of his home, his laid-back life.

"Don't," she said, her shoulders shuddering a little, as if someone had walked over her grave.

He wouldn't, couldn't leave her alone. He touched her with his mind, his memory, his own brand of lore. He thrived on the last modern frontier, a place where farming ruled, where cattle roamed the plains for dinner, and horses still ran wild. Men like him kept the cowboy hero alive. Men like him made women like her believe in second chances.

He said, "Remember how, during the depression era, the president of that time devised ingenious ways to employ the nation?"

"Like the WPA?"

"Yeah," he said, loving the heavy level of their conversation. She'd been in his life for two weeks. Every day of those two weeks had been like the one they shared today: Profound. Meaning and substance penetrated each virgin day, the act defining a bridge of trust between them, a bridge inlaid with stones of accountability.

Miranda took full ownership of each day she lived, and so did he. For him, the past was everything. For her, everything was today. In the time she'd been a guest in his home, he'd learned to treasure the moment.

He said, "Around that time, writers went into former plantation communities and recorded the oral histories of slaves and the children of slaves."

"The slave narratives," she said. "I've heard of them. Zora Neale Hurston had a similar idea when she functioned as an itinerant writer."

He nodded. "You've been traveling across the state doing the very same things. And like Zora, you run the risk of dying unknown, your grave abandoned and unmarked."

"But free."

Pain seized his heart. "What happened to you, Miranda? What made you leave behind the things you must have loved, the people you must have known?"

"My destiny. My purpose. I don't think my life's work is about money or fame or even children. It's to do what I'm doing now, resurrecting and restoring the history of our people. This mission is the force that drives me, feeds me, gets me up in the morning to walk or hitch a ride to the next place on my map."

He could never go back to Carmen. Ever. "Where have you been?" His voice was low and probing.

"I've been specific to the black towns that exist in memory more than paper, towns like Sanders, Rentie, Gibson Station, Wybark, Clarksville, Melvin, Yahola, Lee, Chase, Maybelle, Foreman, Huttonville, Lewisville, and Bookertee. Those places led me to the modern black towns of Tullahasee,

Redbird, Summit, Grayson, Rentiesville, and Taft. Before doing the work for your brother, I'd just finished a job in Boley, Oklahoma."

"Jason told me that. He likes to compete in the annual black rodeo in Boley. He told me that he was there for the event when he heard about your art."

"Yes. He hired me then."

Brody was busy interpreting the facts of discovery into Miranda's life and times. "Taft, Summit, Redbird. I've heard of those towns. They're in eastern Oklahoma."

"Yes."

He pushed her tender spot. "Is that where you're from, Miranda? Somewhere in the eastern part of this state?"

"Like I keep telling you, Brody. Yesterday doesn't matter anymore. I deal in the present. In the present is Abell, not Boley, not Lewisville, but maybe Langston next. Even though the university is there in Langston, much of the town is in disrepair. I'd like to record the way it was during its boom times. In this case, senior citizens are my best source of information. They and their descendents, the people who keep the city government alive. I figure I can make the connection to Langston from Lillian."

Brody was shaking his head in amazement. This was no small task she'd set for herself. To live simply, without the benefit of corporate funds or educational grants, she was living her own dreams, her own unconventional way. He lived his dream, too, which was to preserve the Campbell legacy of training champion horses for racing.

He dedicated himself to keeping his family's land in top working condition. By living his dream, he kept black ranch life in existence. In Miranda, Brody found a woman who appreciated the subtleties of his passion.

Her children, when she slowed down to have them, would be blessed by her alternative point of view. This was not a traditional woman, the reason why he wanted her so much.

This was the kind of woman who anchored a man's hearth and home with domestic structure and a child or two. She was a rule breaker, existing on the fringe of society rather than in its midst. She was an image setter, a powerfully creative woman who had the nerve to walk alone in the dark. Her courage inspired him.

"I've never met anyone like you."

She shook off his flattery. She had little faith in words, preferring instead the truth of deeds. Leonard had said he loved her, and then he'd made a son with someone else. She pushed Brody away. "We're all individuals. To each his own."

"Not all of us are path finders."

She didn't answer for so long, the silence between them grew thick with the questions Brody intended to speak, one by one.

"No," she said. "I guess not."

"You weren't lost when I found you, were you?"

His voice held a note of discovery, with no hint at all of accusation. This left room for truth to be spoken. In the order of his being, Brody required integrity first, honor second in his friendships. There was honor in Miranda's stated mission, but integrity was rooted in the past, something she refused to discuss.

"No."

Suddenly, he wanted to jostle the truth from her. He wanted to make her see him as more than a means to an end. He wanted her to see him as a man she wanted to experience in every way a woman can experience a man. He wanted her in his bed, in his life. "Did you know this was my land?" he asked, his voice more gruff than he intended, his entire person centered on the air she breathed.

She resisted this, his intensity, his attempt to hook and keep her. A man like Brody wouldn't understand the truth of her yesterdays. He wouldn't understand why she'd done what she'd done to Leonard, not just the leaving part, but the complete excision of her past relationships. This was the kind of man who did the right thing when it came to duty and commitment. She had not done the right thing.

Her eyes lost their focus. She knew how to walk a thin line, how to get what she wanted without giving her true self away. She did it by compartmentalizing herself. At this moment, she was an artist, not an escaped wife or a potential lover. This man was her current benefactor, her meal, her board for the night. This setup was all about business. "As in owned by you personally or as in black owned in general?"

He knew she was stonewalling him, but he had all sorts of patience, a talent fine-tuned daily in his passion for healing and training champions. "Both."

She eyed him carefully, this man who played her tit for tat. "I knew about this area in general, the Abell Community I mean, and I wanted to save it for whoever comes next."

"That's what the steno book is about," he said thoughtfully. "You keep a list of the people you've done business with. The names serve the double purpose of being references."

"Yes. While I'm working a site, I find out about other area communities. I've concentrated on black towns that were built before 1890, specifically those areas that are no longer incorporated, like the Abell Community."

"What do you mean by incorporated?"

"Well, black towns had certain things in common, like any city. They had schools, stores, and other formal places to conduct business. Some communities are nearly extinct, which often happened with integration. For instance, in this area, Langston is still a viable, mostly black town, whereas, again, Abell is not."

"You picked my brother Jason's brain about this area didn't you?"

She smiled. He'd figured out another piece of her travel strategy: Make every connection count. "Yes. He told me when I painted the dining room walls for his wife."

"So your wandering isn't random at all." He sounded relieved to know there was a method to her madness.

"No."

In that deep, probing voice of wonder he said, "I don't understand why you stopped fighting to survive. I touched you, Miranda. I know that when I found you, you were willing yourself to die."

"This part of the country is very religious, Brody. Would you believe me if I told you I had offered up all my worldly possessions, and even my soul to a higher power?"

He could tell she was serious. "I would if you hadn't spoken of destiny."

She stared into the distance, her eyes seeing nothing.

"Am I your destiny, Miranda? Is that why you came home with me?"

Her eyes, on his face now, were unreadable. In her silence, he sensed danger, not from evil or injury, but from her long, lovely, artistic fingers, as they stole away with his heart.

# Six

*A Wednesday Morning*

It was Lillian who gave Miranda the history on the section of Logan County where Brody lived, the Abell Community, only they didn't get right to it when they found themselves spending the afternoon alone together. Instead, they got into the platonic discovery of each other, the down-to-the-bone brand of fellowship women will often subscribe to when left to their own devices.

The comfortably dressed women relaxed in red rocking chairs on the wide front porch, each holding a clear glass of sweet iced tea with lemon squeezed into it, a heavy white plate of fresh butter cookies on the square table between them, paper cocktail napkins of autumn leaves used as coasters for their glasses. The men were off doing their own thing, whatever that thing happened to be.

The entire mood on the swept clean porch was down-to-earth, the setting stylish in its simplicity. They were human beings at one with nature, the blending of their separate selves smoothed and shaped by the unconscious as the mind made sense of beauty, texture, and sound in their snug vicinity.

On the weathered wood table rested a cream cotton tapestry, intricate flowers and vines crewel worked upon the fabric in shades of burgundy, wine, and deep blue, each of the colors complimented with variegated leaves of dark jungle green, shot with threads of bright metallic gold.

The artist in Miranda reconstructed the mental imagery of Clive Cussler's fantasy novel *Weaverworld*, in which a tapestry rug was actually a complex and living organism, one composed of civilized people, organized places, and other objects rich in meaning.

Within the tapestry universe of Cussler's classic fiction fantasy, there were worlds within worlds, places where good and evil tangled with want versus need, and every desire was set in an alternative dimension that stretched the limits of what was into what could be.

Miranda sipped her tea and contemplated what was: Leonard's unforgivable betrayal, her art gallery, her upper-class life. She contemplated what is, as in the present. In the present, there were two smoldering fires: the blazing fire of hatred between herself and Leonard, the secret fire of passion between herself and Brody.

She next considered what could be: Real love with a sterling belt buckle wearing cowboy, the kind of man who wore a white Stetson made of straw in warm weather, a black Stetson made of felt in the cold, the kind of man who didn't run from challenge, who played to win. Brody Campbell was her type of man, the type of man who gave her all the room she needed to be herself.

For a deliciously sweet moment, Miranda descended from reality into the welcome spell of the fabric's completeness, a form of stability that was enhanced by the mild air against her unpainted face and the southern sun's late fall heat, which felt just right.

For her, this was the kind of day that was perfect in every way, much like the weave in Lillian's custom linen. It was easy, in that moment, for Miranda to pretend that what was didn't matter anymore, that the only thing that mattered now was what could be.

In order to determine what could be, there had to first be a dream. In Miranda's dreams this day, Lillian was her tried and true friend, Duke didn't spit tobacco juice when he saw her coming his way, and this land, this Campbell land, was the ultimate place she wished to call home.

And what of Brody? she wondered. How would he feel if he knew she had fallen in love with him, something she'd done between the first time he'd kissed her and the first time she'd seen his naked brown chest?

How would he handle the very volatile fact that she was a very married woman, that she would stay married until she carved the time to confront Leonard one more nerve-wracking time? Thinking of Leonard, of facing again that particular piper, forced her troubled mind to reel from the real.

Spiraling headfirst into the magic of make-believe, Miranda fingered the fine needlework, unaware she touched the embroidery with the sort of reverence often lavished on rare religious artifacts.

The detail she studied was intricate and well laid out, a style of workmanship she associated with people who didn't live on the fast track. On the fast track, there was seldom time for the type of highly skilled handcrafting that Lillian had subscribed to on this project. The work could easily be entered into competition with other similar high quality material.

Miranda spoke without planning to say anything special to her companion. "Do you have other table linens like this?"

Lillian had a dozen such pieces in an oversized cupboard in one of the hall closets. "Sure."

"I'd like to see them, work one of them in 3-D somehow, maybe on the wall here above the table."

"Oh, yeah?"

"Yeah."

Miranda could envision the design, too, a table with twin rocking chairs, a lovely crewel-worked linen, a pitcher and two glasses of iced tea, perhaps a basket of flowers at the foot of one of the chairs, a sun bonnet and garden gloves on the seat of the other.

There were so many painting possibilities on Brody's land, far too many for her to start and finish before it was time for her to put on her traveling shoes again. She wouldn't think about that right now, moving on.

Miranda retreated into herself, a self-preservation tactic. Thank God she had her art. In her art, there was freedom to experiment with light and dark, in true life, and in the skewed view of her mind.

As long as she moved from one place to another, she stayed free of commitment. As long as she kept to the back roads of Oklahoma, she would not be found, as long as . . . as long as she didn't give into the urge to share her secrets with Brody.

But then, there was Lillian, and it was clear to Miranda that Lillian didn't mind her own damned business.

As if on cue, Lillian's thoughts rotated around what was said and what was not said, but mostly, she was interested in the fleeting expressions on the itinerant artist's face. The elder woman was convinced that Brody's guest was the most intriguing woman she'd ever met, young or old.

Yes, she was incredibly nosey, but there was no hurry for the juicy tidbits she seriously wanted to learn about Miranda, no hurry at all. The best gossip knew that listening was more important than talking anyway.

With no pressure to do something she didn't want to do or to be somewhere she didn't want to be, Lillian settled into the savoring of the cold, sweet tea, the feminine companionship, the easy blowing breeze against her gently decorated face, the surface of her skin recently dusted with a Revlon brand of translucent face powder.

She thought she looked pretty well pampered and preserved for a woman her age, and in fact, was proud to be a woman her age. She didn't just wish for the good life, the kind of life depicted on the Better Homes and Garden cable network channel—she lived it.

Yes, she was a cook and a housekeeper, but she

was a cook and a housekeeper on a huge ranch spread that had been owned by the same family for generations, a family that had been friends with her family since she was a child.

Oh, this was home all right, because home was where the heart beat best. Her heart kicked into neutral when she entered the cute little cottage she possessed all to her busybody self, a custom-painted cottage that was rent free.

She had unlimited access to each square inch of Brody's land, all in exchange for doing something she loved to do anyway: take care of the people she cared most about. For her, this was definitely the good life.

On Brody's ranch, she didn't worry about what would happen to her when she got too old to live by herself. She didn't worry because in this place, she had the means to survive with the best and the fittest.

She was never alone or lonely, which were the two reasons why Duke stayed on Brody's land: He was living his version of the good life, too. His face was lined by time, but it was lined from the sun, not because he worried about how he'd be living from one day to the next. Like her, he'd found appreciation in this space he called his own.

Lillian attributed much of her unlined facial features to the fact that she knew how to take a good sit on a well-tended porch. On a big porch like this, comfy chairs, sturdy tables and sweet iced tea were necessary items for the relaxation mode she preferred. On a porch like this one, it didn't matter if the rain came down soft or hard, because there was plenty of cover against the elements.

As far as she was concerned, no amount of money could buy the deep-seated satisfaction she felt. She didn't need self-help books to advise her about the surest way to relish her twelve-hour slices of day and night. It was all about the details.

Quality living materialized in the details: Precise seasons. Brilliant stars after dark. Coyotes singing blues. Bending down to smell that gorgeous red rose instead of just looking at it. Life spent in motion as opposed to life spent in regret.

Munching on her third butter cookie, Lillian wallowed in maximum comfort, right here, on this porch, her favorite lookout point, her place of choice to think about all she'd seen and done on any given day. Definitely, this was the good life. For her. Miranda was a different matter altogether.

Could the best secret keeper she'd ever met come to the same idea she had, that home was a place where acres were divided into pastures for grazing, into orchards for canning and selling produce, for gardens filled with vegetables grown free of pesticides, of man and machine working together to benefit the people and animals who depended on them? Could she do it? Could she find a way to love what Brody loved best: this land?

On this land, Lillian lived around people she admired, people who admired her right back. All her needs of food, shelter and companionship were met, and because of this, she had time to think in peace about other people's problems. Miranda's problems. Maybe she needed to come at the girl sideways instead of head on.

She'd already tried it head on and that hadn't

progressed much further than good morning and how's the weather and have a nice day. But that was all right. Lillian liked a challenge as much as Brody did.

Oh yes, yes, yes. Moments like these helped Lillian treasure the rural atmosphere that steered her away from big cities. Besides, there were all sorts of ways for a country woman to entertain herself, gossip being in the top five.

She didn't spend a whole lot of time worrying if the gossip she gave and received was right or wrong, an issue of ethics she solved by trying not to hurt anyone by any of the news she passed along. Inquiring minds had a right to know. She had an inquiring mind.

The way she broke it down was that the field of journalism was full of such people, inquisitive people like herself. The trick of giving and receiving quality gossip was, again, in the details.

Detail number one: Maintain the integrity of the source. Detail number two: Objectively consider the facts. Detail number three: Make sure the topic is relevant in a universal way. Detail number four: Don't be malicious.

Like Miranda, Lillian wound up speaking without thinking first, which, like Miranda, was unusual. "It's great not to live in a rush."

Miranda nodded in agreement. "Where's Brody?" She tried to sound casual but wasn't sure she'd been able to carry it off. She could tell Lillian didn't miss much when it came to her own backyard.

Lillian hadn't missed a thing, the reason she checked her smile. Soon, she'd get to some nitty gritty about the mysterious lady in question. It appeared they were both coming at their information research sideways, which was fine for the preliminaries.

"He went to Willoby's in Guthrie to get the ointment he likes to use when one of the horses has a sore leg. He's got one ailing in the stable now."

Miranda took another sip of her drink and wished Brody was free to join them on the porch. She welcomed the friendship they'd eased into and wanted to expand that camaraderie to include Lillian who was turning out to be balm to all those wounds of hers that were beginning to scar over. Finally.

With Lillian on one side of her and Brody on the other, Miranda felt her fears of being captured by Leonard more in the back of her mind than in the front. Duke was the only fly in the emotional ointment Lillian and Brody slathered all over her every chance they got in the way of careful words and kind deeds.

Easy talks on the porch and gifts of paints and other such supplies were often the order of the day. Still, all that ointment was scraped away as soon as Duke came on the scene. He just didn't like her. Period.

Miranda doubted he'd ever stop looking at her with suspicion. He seemed more interested in his chewing tobacco than he was in her. She had yet to see him smile or hear him say anything nice about her, which made him the exact opposite of Brody.

She spoke once more without thinking first, this time on a sigh. "He's so busy all the time."

"Like most of us. Including yourself." Lillian settled her back against her chair. "Hard to believe you've been here more than a month."

"I know what you mean."

Lillian couldn't resist the urge to delve into the other woman's past point blank. There was so much she wanted to know, especially when today had turned out to be an excellent day for listening.

There was no one else around to interrupt them, so why not get on with her true program: information networking. She saw no reason why she shouldn't stop beating around the bushes.

Being nosey might gain her a clue into why Miranda ended up laid out in the dirt as if she was ready to die. She could pass the news on to Brody so he could stop worrying about Miranda's past catching up to her and taking her away.

If her past caught up with her, which in Lillian's experience the past usually did, then the enigma of what made Miranda live the way she did would not stay a puzzle. Brody wanted to keep his little lovely right where he had her, which was in his house. Lillian knew all this because she'd seen the way his eyes followed Miranda wherever she went.

Although he never told her, Lillian could tell he was falling in love with their cryptic, self-absorbed, highly talented guest. She didn't mind him falling in love. She minded him getting his heart broken by a sophisticated opportunist.

She still wasn't convinced Miranda wasn't dealing them all a rough deal. This thought in mind, Lillian pulled on her invisible leather gloves. She set her tea down on the cocktail napkin, damp now from the sweat off the tall clear glass. She threw the first punch. "You like it here, Miranda. Why don't you stay?"

Deep into her own musings, Miranda failed to notice the cold glint in Lillian's eyes as she took a sip of her tea, her own gaze tracking a pair of young squirrels at play. The animals were mild entertainment in the rustic setting she had fallen in love with the first time she'd witnessed Genesis leading his buddies astray.

Until coming to Brody's place, she'd never thought about the leisure life of animals. Until coming here, she hadn't thought about anything except herself and how she planned to survive from one minute to the next.

Yes, she was cutting a rough deal to her gracious pair of benefactors, but those were the breaks. In real life, wise women looked after their own necks. She preferred not to think about what must have flashed through Brody's mind when he first found her.

All that happened in her yesterdays anyway. Today is what mattered. Today. This moment. This new life. She didn't have to answer to Lillian anymore than she had to answer to Duke Ransaw.

Miranda put her glass down on her respective cocktail napkin. She rested her back against her chair. "Tell me about the Abell Community." Return punch.

Lillian's laugh was deep throated and a tad bit nasty. This girl had guts, which in all honesty, she admired. Miranda made a super sparring partner. Nothing obvious. Nothing physical. Just subtle maneuvering. A feminine cat and mouse game.

"We'll get back to my subject, young lady, but for now," she paused to raise her left brow, "for now, I'll allow myself to be sidetracked."

Miranda stripped her face of thought. "Thank you."

Lillian smiled. "You're welcome. Now. About Abell."

"Yes."

"Around 1947, four local districts, all of them small, fought to keep a rural school open for their area. The Abell family donated land for this goal. The school that was put on this site remained open until 1968. I actually attended an all-black school here that was called Rosenwald. The school no longer stands today, just one of the smaller outbuildings. Sometime I'll show you the school site and the black cemetery that's nearby it. A lot of my relatives and Brody's family are buried there. Most people I know call it Harding Cemetery."

The women were silent a few seconds before Miranda finally spoke. "Do you think desegregation caused the end of the school?"

"That was probably one of the factors. Seems to me like people who live in the country have a fascination with people who live in the city and vice versa. Basically, I'd say that while rural schools made it possible for country kids to get educated on a regular basis, I'd say it's also true that bigger schools had bigger budgets, which meant bigger and better learning aides. I think it was natural for people to want to give their children the best. I've never really thought about it. Probably desegregation both helped and hurt."

"Fair enough. Tell me why you stay in this part of the world."

Lillian's shrug was eloquent. "Well, my people have always lived here. My family tree has Choctaw blood in it. Choctaw Indians lived in this area during the early 1800s. My mother was able to trace her relatives back to the Louisiana Purchase. Her grandparents homesteaded not far from the Campbells when this area was part of the Indian Territory."

Miranda fingered a vine in the tapestry, her gaze on a woodpecker busy hammering away on a steel lighting fixture. Like her, the bird was curious about its surroundings. Like her, the bird was peculiar, eccentric in its behavior.

"I often hear about family roots back to Africa, but I haven't met anyone who can trace her family tree to its Indian roots and still be part of the same land. I guess that's a reason why Oklahoma inspires me so much. Its history is so recent. The Louisiana Purchase happened in 1803. The Indian Territory was designated about, what, thirty years later?"

If Lillian was surprised to be in the presence of a history buff, she didn't show it. Instead, she appeared amused as she refreshed the artist's glass with more iced tea from the nearly empty pitcher on the table. "Something like that."

Miranda used logic to establish chronology. She liked to keep things in order. "Then, Logan County came along in 1889."

"You're talking about the Land Run in '89," Lillian clarified. "This area was part of the Unassigned Lands before it was settled in the Run. It didn't officially become Logan County until 1890."

"What happened to your Choctaw relatives?"

"They got shoved around like a whole lotta folks. Oklahoma ended up being split in half. The west side was Oklahoma Territory, the right was Indian Territory."

Miranda nodded thoughtfully. "No wonder it took so long for Oklahoma to be a state. With so much land up for grabs, it had to be tough to say, OK, we've got enough, we're ready to be a state now."

Lillian shrugged. "I don't know about all that. Basically, one way or another, my Choctaw relatives were booted off their land and ended up in eastern Oklahoma. They became part of the Five Civilized Tribes: The Creek, the Chickasaw, the Cherokee, and the Seminole were the other four nations. There were other tribes, but the numbers were smaller."

"What a mess."

"Yeah." Lillian put her glass down. Her eyes were bright and curious. "Tell me something. Why do you want to know all this stuff? It's not like you're planning on staying much longer."

Miranda fired off her standard response. "Understanding the background of a place helps me set the mood for my work."

Lillian socked away a bit of background herself. For example, Miranda was terrific at saying a whole lot of nothing. "Ah, yes. Your work. You keep painting up a storm and we're gonna end up on Discover Oklahoma."

Miranda laughed. "What's that?"

"A TV show that features special events, foods, landmarks, and neat tourist attractions around the state."

"I'll have to watch it."

"How about this Saturday?"

"Sounds good to me."

Lillian hesitated a moment, leaned forward and said, "But about your art?"

"Yeah?"

"For the life of me, I can't figure out how it works."

"It's all about perspective."

"Go on."

Miranda kept her explanation simple. "The picture has to be centered around one central point. I start out with the big stuff and graduate to littler and littler stuff the closer I get to the focal point of a scene."

"Makes sense. Sort of."

"I also work in depth."

"That's the part I don't get."

Miranda's smile was genuine. "It's pretty easy really. All flat surfaces have only two dimensions: length and width. Depth comes from drawing the viewer's eye to the center of the flat surface."

"I still don't get it."

"I overlap every item in the picture in proportion to whatever it sits next to. I blur the edges with contrasting colors of either light or dark. Items in the front get dark shading. Items in the middle a medium shading. The ones closest to the center point are lightest of all."

"But you do all that free hand."

"Most of the time. That's why I ask so many questions about the location I'm living in before I take on large scenes."

Lillian grasped the overall scheme of things. "The little pictures you've done, like on the fence posts, are like, what, practice pictures?"

"Pretty much."

"Everything is so gorgeous. It's hard for me to imagine you're only practicing."

There was delight in Miranda's eyes as she realized she and Lillian were fast becoming friends. "Writers listen to words. Conversations. They research nonfiction books. They interview people. They observe the details in life. The agonies and ecstasies of it. Eventually, they think and doodle on paper until a story comes together. I do all that too, only I think and doodle with my paints on the walls."

"Wow."

"Thank you."

Lillian believed friendships survived best when kindness and honesty prevailed. She gave and demanded both. "About Brody."

"What about him?"

"I don't want to see him hurt." Punch three.

Miranda shut down. "I'm not into the hurting business."

"Few of us plan on hurting people, but sometimes we do anyway. Just make sure that whatever it is you're running from doesn't catch up with you at his door before you prep him first."

For Miranda, all the easy comfort she'd shared with Lillian was over. They were back to square two and she didn't like it one bit. "I'd leave before that happened."

"When, Little Miss Independent? In the night?

Or would you do it right after he leaves the house in the morning to check on the horses or runs off to meet a client?"

"Let's not get into this, Lillian."

Lillian kept on talking as if Miranda hadn't said a word. "Leaving is gonna hurt him regardless of how you do it. It's obvious he cares a lot about you. A month is a long time when you see somebody first thing every morning and last thing every night with some quality time in between. He's been saving some of his day for you, Miranda. Every day."

"I can't help what he's feeling—or not feeling. I'm just an artist for hire. Really. That's all."

Lillian wasn't pleased with that comment. She let it show on her face and in her voice. "Now, you're lying to yourself."

Miranda hung on to her temper, but it wasn't easy. "I take it you didn't find any negative gossip about me with the Guthrie police or with the sheriff."

"I didn't."

"Then why are you sweating me?"

"If I was sweating you, Miranda, I wouldn't take the time to answer your questions in order to help you get the pictures you're wanting. Me and Duke and Brody take you as is. It's Carmen who wants blood. Your blood."

Some of the tension fell off Miranda's shoulders. She was afraid of no other woman. "I can handle Carmen."

"But can you handle the bone she digs up?"

Miranda scraped all feeling from her face. Perhaps Lillian had only been stringing her along from day one. Maybe all this time she'd only pretended to like her. True or not, the idea hurt. "What bone?"

Lillian got up to leave. She took the pitcher and her glass with her. "The one from the skeleton in your closet."

# Seven

While Miranda sat on the porch with Lillian, Carmen was meeting with one of her friends at D.G.'s Coffee in Guthrie. They sat at a table by the huge front window, a steady stream of traffic running north and south on Division. The steady flowing traffic was soothing to her because it made her think of moving water.

Carmen's friend, a young woman fresh out of law school, wasn't too worried about Brody. "You know he can take care of himself don't you?"

"I didn't ask you here for a lecture, Tanya."

Tanya, a thin, black woman with short wavy hair dyed platinum blonde, sipped her macadamia nut mocha latte very slowly. "Damn," she said. "This is good."

Carmen tapped the table with her French tipped fingernail. "Listen. I didn't ask you to meet me here so we can talk about food, either."

"Lighten up, girlfriend. All I'm saying is that Brody has a great head on his shoulders. Trust him."

"I trust *him* just fine," Carmen said. "It's this Miranda Evans I don't trust. She's just way too invasive."

Tanya laughed. "Invasive, huh?"

Carmen didn't respond.

"As long as I've known you, which has been forever, you've always had it in for any woman you think is more beautiful than you are."

"Why can't I just not like that bitch because she showed up out of nowhere with her hand out?"

"Not true, sister-girl. When you called, I did some prelim work on the phone with a few of my law pals."

"You mean Spud Gurber or Kenneth Gunn." Spud was with the Guthrie Police Department. Kenneth was a former private investigator who had recently moved to Guthrie. Both men were good friends, but she'd wanted a buffer between herself and the truth—that she was jealous of Miranda. It was bad enough that Tanya Tyler knew the truth.

"Yes," Tanya was saying. "Kenneth and Spud. Basically, the woman hasn't done anything wrong."

"She trespassed."

"Brody invited her in the house. She's grown. He's grown. Nobody else is complaining. Let the man go, for crying out loud. You can have any guy you want, Carmen. Why do you have to chase after Brody the way you do?"

The owner of the business interrupted them, a warm smile on his handsome face. "Everything all right?"

The women spoke in unison. "Yes."

"Good. Just let me know if you need anything."

Tanya smiled back. "We will." To Carmen, she said, "Even though I still think you're crazy, I'm glad we got the chance to meet at D.G.'s. I like the atmosphere here."

"Yeah. Right. Back to Brody. He doesn't need to know about this little conversation of ours."

Tanya sipped her mocha latte. She stared at her friend with sad eyes. "Your secret is safe with me, but this is a small town. What you do and say, how you handle your jealousy right now is a very public thing. Don't put Brody in the position of having to choose between you and Miranda."

Carmen stomped her Lisa Sorrell boot. "He loves me. He hasn't known her long enough to want her."

"Just listen to yourself, you evil witch."

"Don't insult me."

"Don't underestimate Brody's good heart, Carmen. He's got this weird thing about truth and justice. I mean, he's fundamentalist about it."

Carmen's grin was malevolent enough to make her tablemate feel uncomfortable. "That's why I want to know whatever there is to know about her. She gave her name. We have a description. She's talented as all get out."

"And beautiful."

"That's not the point."

"You're right, Carmen. The point you need to understand is that this could all go haywire on you and then you'll have even less chance of getting Brody back."

"He belongs to me."

"That man belongs to himself. You can't force him to love you. He doesn't want you for anything more than a friend, which I'm sure he keeps letting your crazy ass know. Attacking Miranda might make you lose even that connection."

"I'll worry about me."

"Homemade jam and fresh pie won't cut it with him, Carmen. Break this, whatever it is you have now with him, and you may lose the most important thing of all—his respect."

In a fit of anger, Carmen stuffed the spent napkins in her Styrofoam coffee cup, but before she could throw the trash away, the owner threw it away for her.

"Look," she said. "I just feel like this woman is hiding something."

"Which she has the right to do. We all do."

"But not her."

"Even her. Especially her. Brody infringed upon her right to privacy. I'd say that cancels out her trespass on his property. You infringe upon her right to privacy by soliciting me to get my friends to go through some back doors on her, get some dirt on her, some kind of crime big and bad enough to make Brody grateful you stuck your fat green nose where it didn't belong in the first place."

"My, my, my," Carmen said. "What a terrific mouth you've got there Granny."

"Only, I'm not the wolf."

"And she's not Red Riding Hood."

Tanya eyed her jealous friend coldly. "What I've done for you is a one-time favor, Carmen."

"That's all I need."

"Is your heart so cruel?"

"I want Brody."

"He doesn't want you."

Carmen didn't say anything because there was nothing to say. She gazed about her, the folk art on the walls and shelves snagging her attention. Paintings by Mike Caldwell. Novelty décor by Dee Stevenson. Books written by a local author. Miranda would want to paint up a storm in a place like this. The atmosphere lent itself well to the creative mind.

How, Carmen mused, could she compete with a woman who painted images in three dimensions? She could bake from scratch, win awards at the Logan County and state fairs, catch her own fish, hunt for mushrooms, trap troublemaking pests like skunks, squirrels, and raccoons. She could ride a horse bareback, shoot skeet, and mud with the best of the best, but all her accomplishments did was make her more like one of the guys.

Not so Miranda. Carmen believed the artist was everything she wasn't, talented in that deeply personal way that could never successfully be duplicated. Miranda could learn to shoot skeet, to ride bareback, but Carmen couldn't do more than paint by numbers.

"He doesn't know what he wants," she said.

Tanya stood, collected her purse, her briefcase. "Good luck."

On the ride home, Carmen smacked her hand on the steering wheel. Before leaving, Tanya had slipped her a sheet of paper with one possible lead. The lead came from Tulsa and was dated yesterday.

All Carmen had to do now was wrestle with her conscience. If she herself was running from something, something so bad she had to get away from home, something she wanted to keep private, did she have the strength inside herself, the courage to strike out on her own with only naked wits and one-of-a-kind talent as her sword and shield? No, she didn't. And this scared her more than anything. But Carmen wouldn't be Brody's friend if her conscience wasn't mostly in tact. So, to be fair, she tried to think of the one thing that could make a tough and talented woman like Miranda run.

A man.

What type of man? Brutal. Cold. Insensitive. Selfish. Domineering. Or maybe the opposite type of man. Passive. Vacillating. Immature. Conniving.

Miranda had to be drawn to Brody, because she honed in on him much too well. His words were like water to her, regardless of how nonchalant, how self-possessed she tried to be in front of people.

Carmen wasn't fooled. A woman understood another woman better than any man ever could. All the secret signals, the double meanings, the veiled challenges and threats. Between women, there was no mystery.

Carmen wasn't suckered in by Miranda's little-girl-lost-in-the-woods routine. No way. She wasn't fooled because Miranda had stood up to her when she knew she was trespassing on Carmen's territory, not Campbell land, but Brody himself.

He wasn't committed to her, but she was committed to him. She'd always loved him, always, ever since she met him in the first grade she'd loved him. But he didn't love her the way she loved him. He loved her the way a man loves a woman he can talk shop with, a woman who liked sports as much as he liked them.

She had finally gotten him to take her serious in a man-woman relationship, but for him, there had been no sparks, just another exploration of the senses with a friend he trusted with his prized possessions: his home, his family, himself.

But, Carmen realized, she'd been too needy, the very opposite of Miranda, who obviously needed other people but was determined to make her way in life on her own terms. As much as she admired Miranda's grit, Carmen also hated her for it. After all, she might spit, shoot skeet, or cuss with the boys, but she'd never wander alone in the dark.

Carmen glanced at the Brighton brand sterling silver watch clipped to her left wrist. It was high noon, butt kicking time.

# Eight

Miranda looked up from the shed wall she'd been studying. She had the urge to paint, only she couldn't make up her mind about what image she wanted to bring into life. During the night, Genesis had escaped and taken a midnight run over the property, the sound of his hooves waking the household as he ran past the bedroom windows.

Brody had chased the horse down in his boots, a white tank T-shirt, and a pair of jeans that were ripped in at least three places. He'd looked good enough to eat right then and there, half-sleep and all. Miranda had wanted to paint him ever since she'd seen him sweet talk Genesis back to where he belonged.

And here was Carmen Oliver, four-time rodeo queen, breaking up her fantasy. The intrusion pissed Miranda off. She didn't bother to keep the aggression out of her voice. "What is it you want?"

Carmen was glad Miranda was in the mood to get down and dirty. If she got mad enough, maybe she would slip and say something damaging. "You."

Miranda rose from her haunches, dusted her hands off and glared at her opponent. She was real tired of being under attack because she made other people feel insecure. It seemed that no matter where she went, people had a hard time accepting that a woman as young and talented as herself would choose to live the way she did.

One thing her back road trekking had taught her was that people tended to mistrust any attitude or behavior that didn't fit with generally accepted stereotypes. For example, some said that most mothers were good mothers, when in truth, some fathers were better at the job of child rearing than their significant others; or that it was OK for a man to take his work on the road, but a woman ought to have a man around to protect her. Oh, yeah. Miranda was real tired of the Carmen Olivers of the world.

She said, "I'm here." She said the words so strong she might have said, "Want some of me? Here it is."

Carmen bounced the aggression right back. "What kind of woman takes up with a strange man, puts graffiti on his walls and stuff like you do, then acts like she owns the whole freaking joint?"

Miranda was surprised to find out she had more fight left in her after all, especially after the go-around she'd just had with Lillian. But then, the more she thought about it, the more she realized what it was that ticked her off the most: Carmen reminded her of Tessa, not the meek Tessa who'd caught Leonard's eye, but the conniving Tessa, the Tessa who showed her true face to Miranda when Leonard wasn't looking.

Leonard talked and talked about his son, but while he'd been busy contemplating the future with his heir, his new bride-to-be had been thinking about the present. In the present, there was an executive-styled home with fine furnishings in it. There was a great looking doctor in his prime, an up and coming man who was exquisitely fit. Tessa had Leonard in the bag all right and the bag was tied up tight.

He was already giving her jewelry, money, whatever she needed in the way of clothes, shoes, and accessories. She had him where she wanted him, which was wrapped around her well oiled and pregnant belly. Miranda figured she might be sticking it to Leonard now, but Tessa would be sticking it to him later.

What Tessa had done was make it impossible for Miranda to stay in Tulsa while the expectant couple stayed in Tulsa, too. Miranda's mother empathized with Leonard, the reason why Miranda had wanted to hurt her mother also. Her father, well, he'd simply supported his tell-him-how-to-eat-and-how-to-drink wife. Together, they were almost as happy about Leonard's baby as Leonard was happy about the baby himself.

Hadn't he bought Miranda's art studio for her? Hadn't he showered her with clothes and gifts and prestige? Yes, they loved their daughter, but they'd grown to love Leonard, too. For them, divorce was about paper, and paper had little influence when it came to separating emotions from duty.

In theory, their duty was to their daughter, but in real life, their emotions were with Leonard. They'd come to grips with Miranda's infertility long ago, not realizing that their son-in-law had not made peace at all. Their hearts had gone out to him—and stayed with him.

But Miranda wasn't concerned right now about the betrayal of her husband or her family. Right now she was concerned about a surprising new discovery: She felt energized by her fight with Carmen. That her sense of self was returning, along with her dormant emotions, gave her a deep jolt of satisfaction.

This time, when Miranda smiled, the smile was real: She showed her teeth. Carefully, she spoke with distinction. "I'm tired of dealing with you."

"Excuse me?"

"You and your arrogance. I won't put up with it anymore. Whatever you had with Brody is over. It's not worth my time to fight."

Carmen stomped forward two steps. She had her demon face on. "I'm gonna get you outta here if it's the last thing I do in this joint." Her voice was low and deadly.

"I'll leave when I'm ready."

"Believe me, you're ready."

Miranda met her toe-to-toe. They both wore jeans, plain shirts and sturdy shoes. They had the right stuff on to get it on. "I won't repeat myself, so listen up, you little ditz."

Carmen's left eye began to tic. "I'm shaking. Really, I am."

"If I wanted Brody, I could have him. The attraction is there. For some women that's enough, women like you who—"

"What do you mean, women like me?"

Miranda's smile bordered on the sly. "Spoiled, selfish, narrow-minded, needy and greedy women. You know. Like you."

Carmen yanked her earrings off, then stuck the jewelry in her pants pocket. "Oh, it's on now, Miss Thing." She shoved Miranda in the chest with both hands.

Miranda drew her fist back, but before she landed a punch, Duke arrived on the scene. He was genuinely amused.

"Ladies, ladies, ladies," he said, "and I use that term loosely, what do you think ol' Brody would say if he caught you hens scratching up those sweet pretty faces of yours?"

Carmen was the first to speak. Her face was tight with anger. "How long you been listening, you old coot?"

Duke spit tobacco juice between the women's feet. They glared at him before stepping back from each other. "Not long as Brody."

The women whipped their heads around.

Brody entered the arena, his gaze directed at Duke first. "You've got to stop all that spitting."

"Seems to me," Duke said in a raspy drawl, "you've got bigger problems than what I do when I spit."

To Carmen, Brody said, "Leave and don't come back."

She hissed at him.

"I mean it, Carmen. Get your things and go."

She actually put a hand to her breast. "You would give me up for this stranger? This, this—I can't believe you, Brody."

"This is my home. You've attacked my friend—"

"Your what?"

"My friend. The friend who's staying in my house

at my request. I want you to leave because I can't trust you to do the right thing while I'm gone."

Carmen knew he was correct, but more important, she knew when to back down. "OK, but I'm telling you, Brody, something about her past is gonna blow up in your face."

"If it does, I can handle it."

Carmen glared at Miranda. "I know you're from Tulsa. Soon, I'll know everything else about you."

"Guess what, Carmen," Miranda said, "I don't give a flip."

Duke made his exit, his eyes delighted as he made sure Carmen didn't torch anything on her way off the property. It had been years since he'd last seen some flat out cat fighting between two grown women. He could hardly wait to tell his friends when they got together to play dominos that night.

Carmen jumped in her truck, her face hot with mixed feelings. In the end, she wished she'd listened to Tanya instead of ruining just about everything except the past between herself and Brody.

He turned to Miranda who looked as if she didn't care what happened next. "You can't keep stirring the pot without telling me what's in it."

"I'm not one of your ranch hands. You can't tell me what to do."

"This is my house, Miranda. Don't abuse the privilege of staying here."

"I'll be gone in fifteen minutes."

"No."

"I'm not one of your horses either, Brody

Campbell. You can't gentle your voice and your hands to get me to do things your way."

"My hands?"

She slammed her mouth shut.

He wasn't having it. "What about my hands, Miranda?"

She looked at him and thought he might be Superman. She felt as if he could see through the wall of her chest, right into the surviving pieces of her soul. She couldn't tell him that when he touched her, his body sent its energy to her, soothing her, warming her.

She couldn't tell him that in his presence she sensed a healer, that in his home, she felt physically restored and mentally revived, resurrected from the emotionally dead. She couldn't tell him, but she could show him.

As if choreographed, Brody opened his arms and she slid into them. In sync, her psyche opened the windows of her desires. The desire for a true home of her own was the most demanding desire of all.

"Oh, Brody," she said, "this will never work." The longer she stayed with him, the greater the threat of discovery. If she stayed, Leonard would find her. She wasn't sure if she was ready for that to happen yet.

Brody's voice was steady and strong. She belonged right there in his arms. "I don't care about tomorrow, Miranda."

"What about yesterday?"

"To hell with that, too."

"Yes," she said softly. "To hell with it."

Brody was free then, free to do something he

hadn't done since telling Miranda he wanted to have sex with her on day one. He tipped her head until it rested in the palm of his hand and he kissed her.

In classic films, one perfectly timed kiss was worth a thousand words, half a dozen explicit sex scenes. It was the purpose of the kiss, the context of it, that mattered most when it came to the first stroke of foreplay. The right kiss held the message of the man.

His was the kiss of a man bent on discovery, a man determined to understand the forces that drove her to paint murals and faux wallpaper in private homes. He was all too aware that with each finished project, she left one more part of her soul behind.

He didn't know it, but with everything that made him one-of-a-kind, he was signing his name all over her heart.

*Brody.*

*Brody.*

*Brody.*

She could almost forget she wasn't a free woman. She wanted to forget. She'd tried hard to put the concept and constraints of marriage behind her, but the law wasn't on her side. The law never had been. Leonard wouldn't rest until he found and destroyed her.

But then, there was Brody. In a show of strength, he picked her up in his arms. In long, determined strides, he carried her home.

"I," she said. "I mean we—shouldn't." She said it, but she didn't mean what she said and they both knew it. She didn't mean it because in this moment, she had her hands on a cowboy, a real man with real needs, a man who wanted the full-package deal—her blood, her sweat, and her tears.

Winding her arms around his neck she said, "You're right. Let's go for it."

They spent hours in Brody's bedroom, lingering, tasting, touching, then lingering some more. Eventually though, after they had played and rested, there was the truth to consider, that without a past, they had no future.

And so it was that as she lay naked in his arms, he said, "I wish you'd just go on and do it. Tell me."

Suddenly, she was tense again. Just like that and the magic was over. "I know. But not now. Not today."

"Tomorrow."

"Yes," she said. "Tomorrow."

She was restless, not for sex this time, but for escape. Leonard had betrayed her, and now she had betrayed him. As of this minute, there were no more stones to throw. She was no longer innocent.

"Lillian must think—"

Brody placed a finger over Miranda's lips. "Lillian knows the difference between her business and mine."

He didn't understand. She didn't want him to understand, but soon, she'd have to tell him everything from the beginning. Soon, he'd tell her to leave and never come back. "What we've done complicates things."

"Or opens them up. The choice is yours."

"And if I choose silence?"

"We both lose."

"Why? Why can't we just be like this?"

"Because I'm not that kind of man. I want you to stay, Miranda. I want you to be mine. Always."

She sighed as if the weight of the world had just landed on her shoulders and her shoulders were about to break. "Come on. Let's, let's—take a shower."

His grip tightened around her body, but in the end, he let her go. It wasn't in his nature to rush things, to force things. He preferred persuasion. Consistency. Quiet, subtle, and constant presence.

She wasn't going anywhere because he wouldn't let her go, not as long as he kept her pampered in the imaginary round pen he'd built for her with his compassion. The round pen was the ranch itself.

All those walls she couldn't resist were the walls of his home, the reason he let her paint anywhere and everywhere her heart desired. She was constricted without feeling restricted.

The balance of the two was an art form Brody had mastered, the art of being a man with the power to whisper to horses until they in turn learned to whisper to him. Until Miranda, he'd never applied this special talent to capture and keep another person.

*Persuasion.*

*Consistency.*

*Constant presence.*

"Trust me, Miranda."

"I do." She might have been a robot set on automatic for all the passion she released in her voice. Every tick of her internal clock brought her closer to doomsday.

In the shower, Miranda made love to Brody as if she might never see him again, as if she needed every soft and hard part of him scorched into her mind forever. Stroking and pumping, he held her until they came together not once, but twice.

She almost told him the truth, right then and there, that she had no right to come apart in his arms, that she was a woman who'd added one more crime to her short list of sins, the crime of adultery. She was going to do it, too, confess everything from start to finish, but for now, she intended to cherish the moment. For now, she had nothing to lose. "I love you, Brody."

"I know."

She was glad he accepted the truth of her words so simply. They were two adults with adult understanding. There was no need to pretend or play adolescent games. Brody wanted her. His protection had nothing to do with love, everything to do with chivalry. Until he discovered her secret, there would be no declaration of commitment, at least not from him. Only fools lived recklessly. He was nobody's fool.

She could ask for nothing more than what she had right now, even though what she wanted was the man himself. No wonder Carmen hated to let him go. He was exceptional. Thinking of Carmen made Miranda want to get away, even if it was only from this room to some other. The kitchen would do. "I'm starving."

He smiled. "Thought I heard your stomach growling."

"You weren't supposed to notice."

"I notice everything about you, Miranda. Everything."

A heavy pounding shook the front door on its frame.

Brody tensed, first with shock, then with anger. With Miranda on his heels, he went to answer the door, flinging it open. It was Leonard, Duke two steps behind him, crowbar in hand. The old man was ready to cut loose.

Miranda couldn't breathe, she couldn't move. TODAY.

Hell was breaking loose TODAY and she wasn't ready. Not like this. Not now. Not . . . ever.

Leonard saw Miranda, his wife, saw Lillian materialize out of nowhere, only to press up behind her, saw Brody taking his measure, heard Duke spitting in the dust beside him and didn't give a good damn. He'd found her. Now he'd kill her.

He said, "I knew I was in the right place when I got to the gate. You painted all over the posts for Christ's sake."

Brody looked at her. "Miranda?"

Her chest was constricted with pain. Her heart, her heart was breaking. She didn't have to worry about leaving her soul in pieces as she created one painting after another, because her soul had shattered when Brody flung open the door.

Her future was now a lonely, desolate place. Brody should have let her die out there in the dirt. If she'd died, she wouldn't feel such pain. Dear God, it hurt, it hurt, but then—she wasn't a coward. She never had been.

She took a long, fortifying breath, then released

it. "Everybody. This is Leonard. I've been . . . expecting him."

No one said a word.

"I better talk to him outside."

Lillian lowered her skillet.

Brody balled his hands into fists.

Duke shook his head.

As soon as Miranda cleared the front steps, Leonard slapped her face. Hard. She hit the dirt. Face down, she was back to the beginning, only this time, Leonard and Brody were flip sides of the same man: Her man.

Brody leapt off the steps so fast Leonard didn't know what struck him. He lifted the Rick Fox clone by the scruff of his neck. He flung him off Miranda who stared at her attacker as if she would kill him if she could do it and get away with it.

The notion shocked Brody, such clear and concise hatred from a socially fractured female. This wasn't the wounded woman who'd been healing under his roof, this was a woman to be reckoned with, a woman he still desired to defend, to keep safe. He hadn't thought he loved her—until now.

But for the moment, all was almost silent.

Mockingbirds mimicked the barking dogs. Two horses whinnied to each other. A heavy truck rattled down the red dirt road running east and west along the property line. Finally, there was the sound of Duke spitting, right in front of Leonard's shiny black shoes.

"Go ahead and get that on me," he said. "Go 'head. See what happens to you. Go on. You country hicks don't scare me."

Duke's voice was low and raspy and full of the menace he held in check. "You're in the wrong place at the right time, mister, to get your face fixed."

"That so?"

Duke's chuckle was a sinister thing to hear. Everybody present wished they hadn't heard it. "Only thing between me and you is Brody."

Leonard's laugh was short and vicious. "Just because I'm from the city doesn't mean I'm stupid."

"What's that mean, Slick?" Duke's eyes narrowed to the danger zone. He was lean, entirely focused. He didn't need much of a reason to throw down. So what if he was seventy something? He was a man wasn't he? Real men didn't watch women get smacked around.

Brody warned Duke off with a look that said, "I've got this." To Leonard he said, "He's right. Slick. I want to hear your piece too, but make it quick. I'm not feeling charitable about now."

Leonard glanced at Lillian. She had the iron skillet dangling from her right hand which was swinging slow and loose, as if she intended to stay warmed up and ready to do whatever she felt was necessary.

Like the men, she hadn't said a word to Miranda, opting instead to form another layer of defense. Obviously, the attack against her was personal, the man who'd delivered the blow someone she wasn't surprised to see.

Leonard struck a relaxed pose. These people didn't know who they were dealing with. "Miranda is my wife."

Brody felt as if he'd been kicked in the chest.

Leonard caught the look. "I see she suckered you, too."

Brody was on him in an instant. The men fought the kind of battle men fight when words are too little and emotions are too much. Even the dogs and the birds and the horses were silent, only the pounding of fist against flesh could be heard. Grunting. Groaning.

Blood.

When the men were spent, both of them sprawled on their butts in the red dust, Lillian said, "Now that's all done, let's get us some coffee. Things are always better after that."

Miranda was poised for flight.

Duke touched her on the shoulder with his open palm. "Don't even think about it. Time's up."

She didn't know why she'd never noticed it before, but it shocked Miranda to discover that despite all Duke's tobacco chewing and spitting, his teeth were stark white. White, the color of truth.

# Nine

The men looked like hell. Whenever Leonard flexed a muscle, Brody tracked him with eyes blacker than any evil. All he needed was a flimsy excuse to land another punch against his opponent, any part of the body would do.

There was nothing about Leonard Evans that made Brody want to get to know him better. He didn't want to hear what the man had to say either, but not listening was childish and inappropriate; so was fighting, the reason he refrained from an act that could only end in disaster. There had been enough disasters for one day.

A pointed glance in Miranda's direction clued Brody in to how very tight she was wired. Even though she worked hard to appear nonchalant, her breathing was almost too shallow to do any good, and her eyes didn't focus on a specific place or thing. She had to be scared to death: of Leonard, of Duke and Lillian, of him.

The only part of Miranda's body that wasn't frozen in place was the bruise swelling on her face, the battered flesh ugly, the sight of it instigating a fresh round of anger in Brody.

What he refused to do was allow his emotions to

get the best of him, because if they did, Leonard would win a minor victory. That wasn't about to happen. Leonard was going to leave his house empty-handed.

Taking note of Miranda again, Brody slowed his breathing and unclenched his fists. He just wished he could unlock his teeth in order to be civil. He would behave in a proper manner.

He would be polite, Brody vowed, at least enough to let the other man sit down without worrying he'd get jumped before his story was told. It was hard though, hard to do the right thing just now. But then, thank God, there was Lillian.

As if she dealt with fighting mad people on a daily basis, Lillian arranged everyone in the formal living room. Brody sat in a club chair, directly opposite Miranda. Between the recent lovebirds was a coffee table, an oversized rectangle that comprised the centerpiece for all the seating in the living space.

On the coffee table was an old-fashioned ceramic carafe filled with Seattle's Best Coffee from D.G.'s. No one drank anything from the assembled Corning Ware cups and saucers.

She'd selected Corning Ware because those dishes were tough to break. The coffee pot was an inexpensive garage sale find that didn't have a defining name on the bottom of the pot.

She figured there was no point in bringing out the best stuff or even the second best stuff for Brody's guest. The man wasn't going to be there much longer, anyway. Definitely, he wouldn't be coming back.

If the pot or the dishes ended up on the floor, she wouldn't mind because they were cheap and easy to replace. Besides, as far as she was concerned, business was business, even nasty business such as this mess tonight.

Of all the reasons Lillian imagined Miranda might be on the run, running from a husband had never crossed her mind, especially a gorgeous, super athlete like the banged-up specimen trying to look cool in the living room.

In exchange for his open cruelty to Miranda, his vicious slap to her face, Lillian had offered him nothing for the pain he must have felt from his various cuts and bruises. She had business to take care of—the business of watching Miranda's back.

Bloody, scratched, rumpled, his clothes ripped in places, Leonard sat alone on the sofa, Lillian on the love seat opposite him. She had put away her skillet, but the pot with the coffee in it was still hot enough to inflict damage against him if necessary.

She was as ready to rumble as Brody and Duke, but she had more class than those two wannabe roughnecks. The hot coffee in the cheap pot was as subtle as poison. She liked to be subtle.

A rabble-rouser of the old school, Duke refused Lillian's efforts to tell him where to sit. If he had his way, the women would be off wringing their hands somewhere while the men hashed out the details of who, what, when, where, and why.

Disgruntled, Duke hauled a chair from the kitchen, which he straddled. For the first time in ages, he didn't have any Royal Copenhagen chew in his mouth. The rusty black crowbar lay beside his dirty boots. The tool was a weapon. Both the tool and the man served as Brody's missile of destruction: armed, dangerous, zeroed in on the enemy. The enemy had a lot of explaining to do.

No one said a word.

Miranda could paint from sun up until sun down, but she couldn't put two thoughts together to explain herself to Brody. It took her a full five minutes to scrounge up the nerve to look him in the face.

When she finally did look at him, she thought her heart might stop. The mask he wore was entirely unreadable. His eyes, through his mask of nothingness, were devoid of expression. It was impossible for her to reach out and touch him: She couldn't bear the rejection if he shunned her.

But ostracize her he did. The weight of his silence, of his slow-burning condemnation was unbearable. It was difficult to imagine that just over an hour ago, they were making love in each other's arms.

In the beginning, she should have told him she wasn't free to love him the way he deserved to be loved—freely. She should have told him that despite the odds against her, that only in his arms did she feel whole again.

But she hadn't had the nerve to do the right thing, and now—she paused to take a long, jagged breath—now she may have lost everything that mattered. What mattered was his love, his deep devotion, his sexual passion, his wants, and his desires.

Miranda had seen Brody kind and warm and giving, but never had she seen him this angry; disgusted, yes, but not this pissed off. He'd been more disgusted with Carmen than angry, but until now, she hadn't realized there was a difference. Having the means to compare had opened her eyes.

Now, it was she he despised, she he most wanted gone. What other reason would he have for staring straight through her, even while Lillian tended to the bruise on her face? Lillian whose touch was gentle, her eyes so cold?

As the true leader of the pack, Brody was the first to broach the question: What to do about Miranda? "Leonard," he said, "you've got three minutes."

Leonard had done his homework on Brody before he arrived and had decided in advance to be direct. Since clear speaking made communication flow best, he didn't bother with diplomacy. "I cheated on her. Looks like she's cheated on me. I'd say we're even."

Brody's nostrils flared. He might have been a bull scraping the ground with his hoof before charging. His voice was cold and rough and mean. He liked the direct approach, but he didn't like the other man's delivery. He and Leonard were men troubled by the same woman, but they weren't the same kind of man.

"That's not why you slapped her," Brody said. The sound of it continued to echo in his mind.

"She took off without a word. Didn't leave a note. I flipped when I saw her with you." It was clear, Leonard was still ticked off. He didn't bother to hide his animosity or his desire to be rid of her.

"If she left," he said, "it's because you did something to hurt her." Thick hatred hunkered low in

Brody's eyes, but his body remained the same, tense and unmoving. His voice was lethal as the crowbar and the pot of hot coffee, cruel as a man with no conscience. He could tell Leonard was lying by the way his demeanor had shifted from something wary to something petty and sly.

"I didn't abuse her."

Brody's voice turned as raspy as Duke's. Coming from a man who was generally big-hearted, a man whose major weakness was that he hated to travel away from home, the raspy sound was a sound of menace. He might have been a dog growling in a show of one-time warning. "What did you do?"

Leonard began to fidget. For a master of communication, a man trained in the art of psycho babble, he wasn't making a connection with Miranda's ready-to-strike wolfhound. The man might be domesticated, but his teeth were those of a wild carnivore. Leonard felt as if he was on the verge of being fresh kill. It didn't make a difference to him if a raging bull did the killing or a raging dog. Dead was dead.

Perhaps, Leonard cleared his throat, perhaps he should take better care with the man of the house. His voice tempered, as did his attitude. "I'm having a baby with another woman. The day I asked Miranda for a divorce, she split."

Miranda jumped to her feet. "God, I hate you." It was as if she could see nothing except Leonard, hear nothing except Leonard.

Duke reached for the crowbar, but Brody stopped him with a glance. "Miranda," he said, "sit down."

She sat.

Brody spoke to the room at large. He sounded used and world-weary, much like the aging, well-traveled Harry Belafonte during a television interview. "There will be no more fighting. Not from anyone."

To Miranda, he said, "Why didn't you do the right things to be free?" The answer to that question was the crux of their entire problem, everyone's problem.

Miranda was so upset she could hardly get the words out to explain herself. These people had cared about her without condition. If only she'd had the chance to explain herself before Leonard got to her. If only she hadn't lied by omission. If only Carmen hadn't been so determined to get rid of her.

If only . . .

Miranda couldn't revisit the past in order to tidy things up for the present. She figured it was best to stick with the facts, those criminal, petty breaches of faith that might very well cost her the love of her life. Her eyes met those of Brody. "Leonard wanted the house, my house to give to her. After seven years of marriage, he wanted his mistress to have it all."

Brody made his eyes flat. This is not what he wanted to know and she knew it. "Tell me."

He would allow her no sidestepping as a means of escape. He didn't care about the length of the marriage or the mistress or the house Miranda didn't live in anymore. All those issues were issues of the past, one she'd walked away from as if it was of no serious consequence, and therefore, those issues were of no serious consequence to him now.

Miranda hated feeling trapped. This time when she stood, Brody didn't tell her to sit down. She paced a few steps and said, "Because of the baby. I can't have a baby of my own." She sounded as if there were no stars left in the sky.

Lillian packed up the coffee pot and its paraphernalia, then headed to the kitchen. "Miranda?" she said.

"Yes?"

"Stop running."

Duke followed Lillian to the kitchen. He hadn't wanted to leave, but he silently agreed with his friend's interpretation of Miranda's way of thinking: Without stars, there could be no hopes or dreams. As old and as ornery as he was, even Duke believed in dreams.

Leonard laughed, but there was no humor in him anywhere. "Congratulations, wife, on gaining such loyalty. These people are clueless about the kind of woman you really are. Didn't think you had it in you to do what you did. Tessa was worried we wouldn't be able to get married before the baby was born."

"Kiss my ass, Leonard."

"Been there. Done that."

Brody felt sick, but he didn't show it. He required balance and beauty and order in his life, but right now, Miranda made it tough for him to be kind. He too, wanted to strike her, and this hurt him almost as much as her betrayal. He'd never wanted to hit a woman, not even Carmen who had been nothing but trouble ever since Miranda had come to stay.

Both women had manipulated him. One because she loved him. One because he loved her. All Brody wanted right now was the truth. For him, truth was more about conformity and convention than emotion. He couldn't, wouldn't allow emotion to get the best of him.

Carefully, he jammed his feelings aside and opened a mental box that said: Logic. "How'd you find her without a paper trail, Evans?"

"One of your locals, a Carmen Oliver, contacted me."

Brody aged three years. Even though Carmen hadn't made it a secret she hated Miranda's guts, he hadn't believed she'd make good on her threats to oust her. Until now, Brody hadn't realized how focusing on his own private pleasures had made him lose touch with the world at large.

Laid back as he was, he'd allowed himself to become a man who worked day and night. Because he enjoyed his job, his lifestyle, he considered his career both work and play. Obviously, Carmen thought he'd been so busy training horses he couldn't see the snake lying in his grass.

But was the snake truly Miranda?

Brody rolled his increasingly bitter, dark gaze over Leonard, Leonard the well dressed man who'd had the gall to tangle with two women and make both of them mad. One was mad because she was married to him. The other was mad because she couldn't marry him at all.

Brody relaxed a bit. Two women and both of

them trouble. He and Leonard had an issue in common: tunnel vision. While each man had been building his empire, he hadn't paid attention to the people around him. People change.

"What do you plan to do now that you've found her?" he asked.

Leonard registered the slight relaxation on Brody's part. He mistook the gesture for one of commiseration. He didn't realize he was still the little lamb lost in the woods. He was the kind of city man who'd never been a Boy Scout. He didn't have a clue which direction was north or south.

He flicked his shoulders in a shrug. "I'll sic the creditors on her. Bet she didn't tell you she has an art gallery."

"She told me what she felt I needed to know." Once he said this, Brody realized the significance of all he'd been given: Her soul. What was her soul if it wasn't her mind?

Her cracked and breaking psyche is what she'd painted on the posts and walls and everywhere else that struck the most secret, sensitive slivers of her separating self. Instinctively, he'd helped her, made room for her to keep the blackened bits of her life in one place—his place. What she had given him was a beginning, the true beginning of faith and hope and trust. She just hadn't had the words to tell him, she'd only had her art, a quiet skill that had won him over.

Leonard shrugged. "Look man, believe it or not, I've never hit my wife before. Didn't plan on doing it today, but I saw her with you and lost it for a second. Her parents think she's dead."

Miranda couldn't face Brody. What must he think? How sorry he must be for having saved her. Her heart was spinning so uncontrollably, she felt it easier to confront Leonard instead of him.

It was easy to confront a man who profited on other people's pain. Leonard's career path had been about money. Leonard was always about money. So was Tessa. Perhaps—Miranda took a long, satisfying breath—perhaps justice would be served after all.

She was surprised her voice was so calm. As long as Brody stayed in this room, there was hope. As long as there was hope, there might still be another chance to find love in his arms.

"I expected you to close the gallery. You never appreciated the work I did there. I figured you'd get rid of my stuff right away." She was genuinely curious.

Leonard wasn't fooled by her calm. There was a hellion sitting in that chair. "I wanted to, but after your parents went to the news about your disappearance, people started coming by the gallery. Your work sold like crazy. There's a list of people who want to commission you. After all this time, you've got money in the bank. Your gallery manager kept the day-to-day stuff going."

Miranda was clearly shocked.

Leonard's laugh was an honest one. "I don't believe it, either, but anyway, it's true. You've become an overnight success in Tulsa."

For a moment, the trio were at a loss for words.

Brody stood. "Look Evans. Nothing is gonna get finished up tonight. Where are you staying?"

Leonard rolled his shoulders, massive from his many workouts. "Somewhere local. Make a suggestion."

"The Best Western off the interstate. Directions are easy from here. We'll meet you in their dining room tomorrow morning at 10:00."

"No problem."

Leonard raked his eyes over Miranda. She looked battered and hurt and he knew it was his fault. He never intended to slap her, but once his hand connected with her face, the moment felt good. He'd wanted to avenge himself, even if the gratification he felt was short lived. The entire situation was rotten, inside and out. Still, he had cared for her . . . once.

"I'm sorry," he said. "For everything."

Lillian materialized from the kitchen to walk him to the door. Duke took the lead from there by escorting Leonard to his car, giving him directions to the hotel along the way. He didn't bother telling him which way was north and south.

After Leonard was gone, Duke returned to the living room where Lillian, Brody, and Miranda were waiting in silence.

The old ranch hand returned with chew in his mouth. His eyes sparkled with mischief. "Hot diggity damn, girl."

Brody looked at Miranda too, but there wasn't admiration in his eyes. There was consternation. "Yeah. Damn."

# Ten

Thirty minutes later, Brody and Miranda sat by themselves in the solace of the kitchen. They had nothing to eat or drink, the reason the table between them was bare. This was not a pleasant situation for either of them. It was simply necessary.

Miranda scarcely kept still for wondering what Brody might say next, what he might do once their conversation worked its crooked way into some kind of awkward groove.

After Leonard was escorted off the property, she'd returned to her room to pack, but once she'd closed the door behind her, she hadn't been able to make up her mind what to take.

In the end, she chose nothing, not her paints, her list of references, her scant cache of clothes, nothing. She hadn't felt this insecure about the future since leaving Tulsa, and even then, she'd been inspired by anger. She wasn't angry now. She was scared.

The force of her feelings frightened her into thinking every second she spent in this kitchen might be her last. It was so quiet, unnaturally quiet, as if even the birds and the night animals understood that danger was near.

How to stretch the eternity between each tick of the clock, knowing that at the stroke of the next hour, she might be on the road again, not in search of salvation this time, but in search of some solitary place to apply the proverbial tongue to her various wounds?

She'd slash ten years off the end of her life to start again at the beginning, to make friends with Carmen, to come clean with the people she'd left behind in Tulsa, to give thanks to those who'd purchased the art in the gallery she still missed.

She'd forfeit another ten years to see the man she adored gaze into her face with a lover's sweet, sensual desire. To feel once more his naked embrace, his beating heart against her soft, tender breasts.

If . . .

Dear God.

If . . .

When Miranda could stand the strange silence no longer, she said, "Looks like we're going to be up pretty late. I mean. You know. Like the first night."

Only this time, she was a wreck and it showed. Her face, bruised and pinched, held no secrets. There was no other place to hide, not behind her own façade, nowhere. He knew her now.

He knew the way she smelled, the way she kissed, the way she responded to love and to making love. He knew she was a sinner, not a saint. She had violated common and religious laws: a sinner. She was neither patient nor unselfish: not a saint. She took what she wanted, be it freedom or a place to paint.

Some might say she was reckless. Some might call her a hero.

Brody had the grace to answer her, although it was clear she'd cut him deeply. The pain was there in his eyes, obvious, eloquent, quite easily everlasting. If he wanted to take her in his arms, she couldn't tell.

"Seems so." He might have been Clint Eastwood in a rugged western film, Mario Van Peebles in the movie *Posse*. His attitude was neither here nor there. Oh, but what did he see?

Miranda's emotions strained for release. It took maximum strength to maintain what dignity she had left. In her misery, she found it difficult to see her own, carelessly guarded self-worth near ruin. Her inner world was gray. Dark, dull. Black and white. Gray.

There were other men, other towns, other images to paint if she cared to look. Only she didn't want other men, she didn't want to see other towns, and if she never painted another stroke, then so be it.

For the first time since discovering she would bear no children, she stopped worrying about her physical imperfections. On Brody's land, there were mothers with foals to bring into the world, not once, but many times. If she stayed, she'd be around to witness new champions in the making.

But what of her own champion? What of Brody?

God, he was handsome, austere and solemn in his hard wooden seat, bitter as cheap coffee. His hair was short and black, complimented with natural waves. His eyes were somber, his lips full, yet firm, kissable, only he didn't want to be kissed.

His jaw was as yielding as stone. How would this

hard-working cowboy ever find it in his heart to forgive her?

She wasn't sure if he had it in him to turn the other cheek. She was an outlaw, a woman on the run, a woman who hadn't played by the rules, a vagrant, an outcast, a damsel who'd created her own distress.

If she had any pride, she would have left with Leonard so they could head back to Tulsa in order to finish their nasty business, but she didn't have the nerve to leave that last bit of her soul behind, because that last piece was the center of her character, the right and the wrong of her, the good and the bad.

The black.

And the white.

If she had truly loved Leonard, she'd have fought Tessa to keep him. She hardly knew Brody and had fought Carmen from the start. She'd made a place for herself on Campbell land. If she hadn't taken to the road, she'd never have found this heavenly sanctuary.

Yes, Leonard had found her, but only because she had reached her destination. Miranda squared her shoulders. To hell with crying.

"I'll start from the top," she said.

"Seems appropriate."

Miranda eyeballed the man of her dreams and knew this was going to be more difficult than any peril she'd ever faced. He might take her back, but damn him, he was going to make her break a sweat first. "I ran away because of the baby."

"You said that."

Such cruelty. She wanted to reach out, touch his

face with her hands, sit on his lap even, but she'd never been that kind of woman, the kind to beg. She hadn't promised him the actual truth beyond her spoken name, she'd only promised him the day they were living, one moment at a time.

At least in this, she hadn't lied. This had been her integrity. She wasn't going to flip the program now. She just had to get time in motion for them again. She had to find the words that would begin the healing. Forget eternity, the happily ever after.

What did eternity mean to her if there was no here and now? There was no innocence here this night. She wasn't pure nor would she ever be. She was guilty, guilty, guilty, but she would not bend to the censure swirling around her heart and soul. On this one night, she would open the doors of her desires and keep them open for Brody to either accept or discard.

One night. This night.

She spiked her chin in the air. This was a man before her, as human and frail as herself. There were crimes far greater than hers, which had been and still was, a method of survival, survival of the fittest. If she wasn't fit, she would have died.

"I wanted to pay Leonard back for what he'd done."

"Mission accomplished."

His eyes, she noticed, were marble tough. She had the impression he wasn't blinking, even though she knew for a fact he was doing just that. The entire effect of him, his cold black eyes, his carved empty face, his immobile body, all set her nerves on end.

So what if she had butterflies? She was still brave.
She was still the heroine in this story, her story, and
in this tale, he was the prize, her reward for stepping outside the box. This made him worth the
fight.

Even though the dark of loneliness beckoned,
she'd walked alone in the dark before. She could
do it again if she had to do it, but she wasn't giving
up on hope just yet. His was the light that had
helped her see again. Every artist needed a bright
and shining light.

She tried again. "I guess I was ticked off at the
world, more hot with Leonard and my folks than I
was mad at Tessa. She was just looking out for herself."

"And the baby?"

"You mean, Leonard. Leonard, Junior."

Brody blinked slowly, but his face didn't budge
an inch toward forgiveness. Like the cowboys of
myth and legend, he was built of raw, brutal
strength. Yes, he whispered to horses for a living,
was gentle and loving, but he was still a warrior at
heart.

Could she blame him for fighting the urge to tell
her good-bye? No. If the shoe was on the other
foot, she'd have a hard time going with the flow her
own self. She was thankful he was at least listening,
especially when he was almost too hurt, too angry
to be civil.

How many men would have cut their loss and
considered themselves lucky to be rid of a broken
woman? Dozens. But Brody was not an ordinary
man. Ordinary men didn't talk to wounded, fright-

ened horses or win their souls with understanding. Or women.

His compassion showed in the shift of his verbal position. "That has to be painful, knowing the baby's name up front. I'm sorry this happened."

He might have been a barkeep being kind to a drunk along a solid strip of dark and gleaming mahogany. Public courtesy. Nothing personal.

She didn't care about the cool avenue he'd chosen, this was her grand opening, so she took it. Struggling for calm, even faked calm, she strove to keep her voice on an even keel as she bit the brass bullet.

"Do you forgive me?"

He honestly didn't know what to say. How could he tell her he had moved away from anger to jealousy? He didn't want a rival, but he had one. Leonard was cash rich. Only a man with money to burn would juggle two high-profile, high-maintenance women.

Brody was land rich. He owned miles of property, lived in his ancestral home, hobnobbed with wealthy animal owners and lovers near and far, but he drove a dusty Chevy, not a sleek, expensive sedan. He didn't wear a Secret Agent Man watch.

Leonard was married to Miranda. This bond, their history, made him a powerful adversary. How did he know that her escape wasn't a ritual between two volatile people? He didn't. How did he know he wasn't a pawn in some twisted, marital game of cat and mouse, hunter and hunted? He didn't.

Leonard was Miranda's man.

Hidden, secret, but always there.

Brody's jealousy blackened his heart, turning him vindictive. He had already struck his rival. Even now, his animosity was a force against Miranda, whipping her intellectually, cursing her silently, striking her emotionally. This was his dragon: this all consuming, destructive jealousy.

He was trapped by love. Still, he had to fight. Against his jealousy. Against her betrayal.

They stared at each other, carefully, tragically. A chasm of hopelessness existed between them where once, only trust had been on the table.

"Speak your mind, Brody."

He wanted to tell her that as crazy and messed up as she was, he still wanted her to be a part of his life. He just couldn't bring himself to say it. Perhaps it was pride. Perhaps it was old-fashioned, common sense, self-preservation at its fundamental best. He had no words for all he felt. He was a man of action, not one of introspect.

Miranda felt tears threaten, but she held them back. How could she hope he would forgive her? A man who valued his family and home the way he did wouldn't begin to understand the mind-set that made her flee Leonard. She'd do it again the same way if she had that fateful day to begin brand new.

If it was clear to her that she wasn't sorry, it had to be clear to Brody, as well. Maybe this was it, after all. Maybe this really was good-bye and she was too stubborn to let go with class.

"Say something, Brody. Anything."

Finally, he latched on to the thought that stung the most. She hadn't just betrayed Leonard, she'd betrayed everyone in her life. "I can't get over your family thinking you were dead. I can't believe you have an art gallery. I can't believe I'm in this mess. I don't know you, Miranda. I never did."

She sighed in relief. Now, they were getting somewhere. As long as there were words, even angry words, they had a chance to pull things back together. "I'm not proud of what I did." At least that much was true.

"You aren't sorry about it either, are you?"

"No."

He leaned a fraction forward. His left eye jumped with blood. Twice. "What about your parents? Why didn't you send word to them that you were all right?"

He couldn't imagine his parents thinking he was dead, not when a phone call was so cheap and easy.

Her shrug was matter-of-fact. There was no point in pretending she hadn't shafted her family when she jumped on the mythic empty freight car on the fastest train to Anywhere, USA.

"If they'd been supportive in the first place, I'd have gone to them when I left Leonard. They were part of the problem. I guess, well, I guess something inside me just . . . snapped. When it did, I decided there'd be no more tears for me."

"As in no regrets."

"Yes," she said, lifting her chin a little higher. "That's it exactly. See, at first, I couldn't believe Leonard would do such a thing. With all the homeless children in the world, why couldn't we have adopted one? No, he couldn't do that, adoption wasn't real enough for him, so he went off and made a baby with Tessa. He made a fool out of me, Brody."

"So you made a fool out of him in return."

This wasn't a question. He was laying a new road down, point by point, fact by fact. But where the road would lead, he wouldn't know until this night was done. Tonight was all about going the distance, together, if possible. He had to decide if she was worth the risk.

At sunrise, it would be tomorrow. Tomorrow was the future. He couldn't afford to be kind or gentle. He couldn't afford to bend. He'd done enough bending already. She would never be able to hurt him again the way she'd hurt him by keeping her past a secret.

Some secrets were never meant to be kept. She'd been wrong and nothing short of forgiveness could make things right again. But he had to try, it was the only way he could look back on this night without regret.

He said, "Keep talking."

She almost called him a bastard. Her eyes glittered with something, what, he didn't know. "Leonard is religious about appearances. Every hair in the right place, every muscle in tip top shape." Her face twisted in disgust. "The lousy liar."

Brody leaned back the fraction forward he'd taken into her space. His eyes, still hard, still cold, assessed her as he might assess stolen property. She was definitely stolen goods. Leonard's goods. Contraband.

"You've got a lot of feeling left in you, Miranda. Do you still love him?"

"No."

"Good."

For the first time, she relaxed. His voice had mellowed, the change so small she would have missed it if she hadn't been looking for it.

"I'm sorry, Brody. I'm sorry you had to find out this way. About Leonard I mean."

Dignity and wonder rivaled for a spot on his face. "I've never made love to a wanted woman."

She smiled about the wanted woman part. In her small circle of friends in Tulsa, she must be notorious. "No. I suppose not."

He ran a palm around the base of his neck. He flexed his shoulders. Neither move released his tension. "On the one hand, this is complicated. On the other hand, it's not. Lillian is right about one thing, you don't have to run anymore. Leonard put a stop to that."

"I'm relieved its over."

"Because you want to stay or because you don't have to look over your shoulder anymore?" There was a deepness to his voice that hadn't been there when they first sat at the table together once Lillian had gone to bed, frying pan in hand, just in case.

"Both."

In less than three hours, there would be daylight. The time to be cold and macho was over. Brody had to leave a hole in the road he was paving and move on. Some things could only be patched, never properly fixed. This was turning out to be one of those things. Real heroes didn't hold grudges. They lived their dreams.

"I understand now why you refused to talk about the past," he said. "You couldn't afford to let anything slip. Even though I understand, I'm angry you didn't trust me with the truth."

She flung her hands open in a what-will-be-will-be gesture. "Once I took off, I didn't want to stop moving."

Reasonable by nature, Brody studied her point of view with an open mind. "You were stuck in an ugly situation. I don't condone what you did, especially to your parents, but I don't condemn you for it, either." It was a start.

Miranda eyed him with a deeper level of respect. There he sat, strong and fine, angry and concerned all wrapped together. Instead of being an obstacle to deal with, he'd made himself her ally. His knowledge of her predicament was an asset instead of a liability. It felt good not to be alone.

He was not a man she could forget, nor was he a man she could easily walk away from, as she had walked away from Leonard. In the time she'd known Brody, he'd made her feel every subtlety of peace: mental tranquility, physical tranquility, spiritual calm. He'd given her a place to rest her body and her mind.

In his company, she'd found a cessation of war, the war between what she couldn't have and what she could. She couldn't have a baby, but she could have a love that would last her for the rest of her life—if only they could survive this night.

In her absence from Tulsa, her art had taken on a life of its own, selling because of her and without her. The negative of her departure had produced a positive result. Since leaving the turmoil of Tulsa, she'd found order, cultural purpose, and personal harmony. Once more, the positives outweighed the negatives.

The eyes Miranda turned on Brody, her lover, her soul mate, were eyes of decision. "I want to stay with you."

He smiled without thinking about it. "Why?"

"Because I love you." There, she'd said it.

He loved her too, but he wouldn't say it. He couldn't say it. When he worked with his horses, all he thought about was her. What was she painting? What was she thinking? When would she leave him? How would he live without her?

All his nightmarish musings were realized by hard knocking at his front door, of Leonard coming after his wife.

Leonard. The enemy. The rival. The villain.

For Brody, holding back was about personal responsibility. Born and raised in the country, trust was imperative. People didn't lock their doors at night because they believed in their neighbors. People left expensive horses with him because they had faith in him. Once broken, trust was a difficult quality to earn back.

"I don't trust you the way I stopped trusting Carmen. I can't leave her alone with you. I can't expect you to stay. Two sides of the same coin."

She felt stricken. Sick. The parallels were too close for comfort. He was right. "I'm sorry."

She stood from the table, but he caught her hand and she sat down again. Why rush the bitter end? She'd much rather savor the pain to nurse later, the agony and the ecstasy of having won and lost her one true love.

His concerns were valid ones. "How can I know that when you get upset around here, you won't pack up and leave? I won't walk on pins and needles trying to keep you happy." He had a business to run, a reputation to keep. If he spent half his time worrying about her, he'd be half the man he was before he met her.

In turn, she wasn't going to make promises she couldn't keep. For all she knew, he might decide to run off with Carmen some day. Anything was possible. "What happened to me and Leonard is what happened between me and Leonard. You and I are two different people."

"People who run once might do it again."

This was going nowhere. "Like I said, I'm not one of your horses or one of your ranch hands. You've got to deal with me using what you know about me. I wasn't a fake. I was just showing you the sides of me I wanted you to see, the sides of me I wanted to be."

His voice was quiet. "I understand."

She opened the floodgates of reason and reveled in honesty. "I realize now that I can't shut out the past anymore than I can stop the future from coming. What can I say, Brody, except that I love you? I love this house. This land. I've learned to live without tears because of the woman I am today. A life on the road helped me find the backbone to be free."

His heart was in his eyes, stamped on his face, but to say the words—he couldn't do it, not yet, not this easy. "But that's just it, Miranda. You aren't free. You never were free to leave Leonard the way you did. It has to be finished."

"In my mind, I'm free."

He scoffed at the idea of freedom in this situation. She'd formed a legal partnership that hadn't been terminated properly. That was his bottom line. "You live in the real world. Don't pretend your marriage and vows were minor issues. If they were minor, Leonard wouldn't have tracked you down."

Miranda felt a million and one degrees of anger. Leonard followed her in anger, just as she'd run away in the same sort of temper. They married because they were in love and had things in common. For whatever reason, they had fallen out of love.

Time on the road had helped her come to grips with reality, and not all of it was black and white. Brody wasn't being fair to only consider the obvious problems of her defection from Tulsa.

Even though she wasn't present, there was another woman with as much to gain as Miranda. Tessa wanted prestige. Instant success. Instant trophy wife status in a house full of high-dollar fashion statements.

Miranda might be a bitch in this drama, but she wasn't the only bitch. She tossed her shoulders back. She and Brody might part ways forever after this fiasco played itself out, and if they did, she'd leave with her head high, even if her butt was banging the ground. She survived Leonard. She'd survive Brody, too, even if the cost was high.

"Tessa wants to be married before her baby is born. That's why Leonard is here. The main reason, anyway."

Brody's expression said there had to be more to it. "There are financial burdens as well. You left him in a trick bag."

"I'll pay the piper, Brody, but I'm not sorry for

what I did to Leonard. He deserved it then and he deserves it now."

"Do you despise him that much?"

"I do."

Maybe Brody was disappointed, maybe he wasn't. Not every fairytale had a happy ending. There were monsters in this tale, the monster of envy, the monster of greed, of pride and yes, even of loneliness. No one was innocent.

He spoke as if he'd received divine revelation. "All that painting you did was your saving grace."

"Maybe."

His tone turned brisk, businesslike. This interlude was nearing its end. "What do you plan to do about Leonard?"

"As in step one?"

"Yeah."

"Divorce him."

Business question number two. "What about your gallery?"

"Sell whatever is left."

"The debt?"

"Leonard paid for everything we had. I owe him a trip to a lawyer. I took the only thing that mattered and that was my work. I am the work."

*I AM.*

Revelation cracked the ice around Brody's heart. *THE WORK.*

How could he have been so blind? So stupid? He'd been worried about her leaving pieces of herself behind with every finished project, never once considering that she was a piece of the work itself— a work in progress.

He laughed outright and his laughter shocked her. Dare she hope? Dare she retrieve her dreams one last time? Yes.

Her voice a whisper, she asked, "What is it?"

His smile was a crooked one. "The irony of all this. Some people would think I'd be a fool to let you stay. I'm one of those people."

"I've been a fool and survived."

He took both her hands in his own. The connection felt good. "You're referring to your marriage."

"I am. Tell me something, Brody. When have you ever cared about what other people think?"

His ironic, crooked, unwilling smile was a dangerous thing to her hopeful heart. If only he knew how much she loved him. Like the paint on the walls, he had no idea of the magnitude of all she'd given him, all he'd given her.

"Today," he said. "I started caring today."

"Touché."

He massaged her fingers. "I don't know what's worse, watching you act as if you don't care what happens, or watching Lillian watch me watching you."

Miranda was taken aback. "Lillian?"

"She told you to stop running, remember?"

"I remember."

The marble was back in his eyes. Black eyes. All seeing eyes, and yet, there was no animosity. "She was also telling me she thinks I ought to let you stay."

"Wow."

"Yeah. Wow."

Miranda squeezed his hands. This might work. It just might. "You don't find my infertility a problem?"

In all this time, Brody had never seen her look or sound so vulnerable. He almost pulled her into his arms, but he wasn't about to let his emotions get the best of him—or her. Not yet. "It's always a problem for people who want to have children. It's a natural extension of being married."

"You didn't answer my question." She sounded breathless, as if she couldn't take a full breath if she tried. He bet she couldn't.

His voice was soothing and gentle. "I don't think it has to be a problem. I want children, but children right now are beside the point. I want you, Miranda, but not like this."

"I am who I am."

"And so am I."

Slowly, she pulled her hands back. "Now what?"

"Some distance."

It was her turn to wear eyes of stone. "Women are a dime a dozen for men like you. Once I'm gone, you'll get over what happened."

"Men like me believe in truth and honor. Nothing is what it was between us. I want you, and I resent you for making me want you."

He had a right to feel cheated. "You gave me a clean slate. I love you because you gave me a chance to find out who I want to be. What I want to be."

He held his breath a few seconds. "And what is that?"

"Your woman. I want to stay here with you."

He didn't say a word. How could he, when Leonard was staying at the Best Western, waiting impatiently for the light of morning to come.

Miranda wanted to weep.

# Eleven

She got up to leave the table, but he wouldn't let her go. "Come on," he said. "Let's get out of here."

"It's almost midnight."

"Our witching hour."

She couldn't believe this was happening, this spontaneous leap of faith, but she welcomed it. She welcomed him. "Shall we walk or ride?"

"Let's ride."

She laughed, the sound of it full of incredulity. She had thought it was over. She thought Leonard had won. "Genesis is gonna love this."

Genesis did. It didn't take long for them to saddle the horse for their moonlit ride. The sky was bright from the moon, the stars dim around it. The night sounds enveloped them, as each drowned in the touch and emotion of the other.

Miranda rode in front of Brody, her body nestled firmly between his thighs, the muscles of his legs powerful beneath his rugged Levi jeans. She rested her back against his chest, her eyes open to the earth and its mysteries of the night. This was home all right, if only she could convince the man who held her so tenderly.

She had done nothing to make him happy, and

now she wanted to do everything she could to bring him some of the joy she'd felt at finding sanctuary in his home. His friendship was worth the risk of her dignity. "We've got to make this work, Brody. Cinderella didn't let the prince get away."

He couldn't resist the urge to press his nose against her hair. It smelled good. "It was the other way around wasn't it?"

She knew he'd captured her scent and was glad she hadn't murdered Leonard the way she'd wanted to back in Tulsa. She was glad that she'd taken her talent and her wits and her will to the back roads of Oklahoma because if she hadn't, she'd never be where she was right now, held tight in the arms of a man who loved her, on the back of a horse named Genesis.

*Genesis: The first book of the Old Testament.*
*Genesis: The act of originating.*
*Origin: The beginning of the existence of anything.*
The first.
Original.
Birth.
The horse stopped its forward motion. They were on top of a hill. Below the hill was a creek. Beside the creek was a bench. The path leading to the bench was wide and well trampled. Brody slid of the horse's back. Miranda slid into his arms. He squeezed her tight, then let her go.

She said, "I didn't know this place was here."

"There are a lot of things you don't know."

She wasn't sure what to make of his statement, but his tone was loose and easy enough that when he offered her his hand, she took it. Together, they walked to the bench. The night sounds were loud. There was the rustling of small animals nearby, but the peace, the bright moon, and the company were just right.

Miranda sat beside him, their thighs touching. He was still her hero, more now than when he'd found her. True heroes didn't run when hell broke loose.

He was angry, yes, but he was also a man schooled with reason. Only a fool walked away from destiny. She'd be a fool to walk away from him. "If I were a singer," she said, "I'd write a song about you."

He turned on the bench, so that she rested her back against his chest, her head falling against his shoulder. This time, he did more than take in the scent of her hair, he used his cheek to caress her face. The silk of her skin was erotic. "Why write a song, when you can paint?"

She shivered a little, not from the chill of the night, but from the heat in his voice. The timbre of his tone poured through her, dark and sweet, it spoke to her in her special, secret places, all the places he had once been and, if she had her way, would be again.

"All the best songs say what the average person can't put together in a few short lines," she said. *Reasons* by Earth, Wind & Fire, *I'm Only Human* by Jeffrey Osborne."

He nuzzled her neck. "*Let's Get it On* by Marvin Gaye."

Her laugh had a catch to it. She hadn't expected to find herself making out on a bench in what was turning out to be a secret garden, their own private garden of Eden. "*Smooth Operator*," she said. "Sade."

"*Tell it Like it Is*. Aaron Neville." He adjusted her

on the bench, and kissed her. When he got tired of kissing her, he laid her across his arm, opened her shirt and took his pleasure there, too.

She came up for air and said, "*Ooo La La La. Teena Maria.*"

He took a deep breath, then let it go. He wasn't about to make love on a hardwood bench. As soon as they took their clothes off, they'd be nibbled and munched on by all sorts of things they couldn't see, things he knew lived in the grasses so close to the water. "Let's finish our ride."

"You're making me crazy you know."

"We're getting even then."

"This is a Brody I've never met."

"What do you mean?"

"No holds barred, Brody. Ruthless Brody. Got me all wired up and wet with no place to spin my wheels, Brody."

"I'm not done with you yet."

"I can't tell if you're threatening something good, or relishing something bad."

"I don't plan on loving you tonight and kicking you out in the morning if that's what you're thinking."

"I'm not sure what I think. I know I want to sleep with you in your bed for whatever is left of the night, but after that, I don't have any specific plans. I can't plan until I know what you want to do about tomorrow."

"We'll deal with tomorrow when it gets here."

On the ride back to the house. Neither of them said a word. All the doors between them were open. Through the open doors were opportunities lost and opportunities to gain. Once they made love tonight, past and present would roll into one great scene of commitment.

Once they made love, Brody wouldn't be able to throw her past in her face, because by taking her in his arms again, in the absolute privacy of his inner sanctum, his bedroom, he'd be accepting her as the married, lying, shattered woman she had always been.

His weren't the only eyes that were open, once he accepted her, stamped his seal of commitment on her, then he would also demand some sort of restitution. Yes, she'd gained his love, but she'd also lost his trust.

Miranda pressed the night light on her wrist watch. It was 3:00 A.M. Restitution was at hand: The piper had arrived. She wasn't ready, but she had to be ready. She wanted time to slow down, but time slowed for no one.

In a few hours, she'd meet Leonard alone at the Best Western. She'd ride with him to Tulsa. In Tulsa she would deal with her notoriety, close her gallery, pack and sort the remains of the woman she used to be. She'd do it all right this time.

She'd stay gone long enough to give Brody time to think straight. After all, the sun was rarely kind to secrets or to secret keepers.

*Stop the World Tonight.* Percy Sledge.

But the world didn't stop.

Miranda's day of reckoning began in perfection. She dressed simply, in jeans, a blue sweater, and a pair of boots, all gifts from Lillian, who kept dashing tears from her eyes.

Duke was driving her into town. There was no spitting, no Royal Copenhagen. He wore a long-sleeved checkered shirt, creased jeans, and dark brown patent leather shoes. His hat was as black as his mood as he watched her say good-bye to Brody.

Brody wasn't the kind of man who wallowed in what ifs. He bent his face to Miranda's and simply breathed the air she breathed. He liked the way she smelled, fresh and light. Only the bruise on her face reminded him of the battles she had yet to face, battles she had to fight alone.

For the long good-bye, he wore a fresh pair of Levi jeans, stonewashed. His shirt was short sleeved and vanilla colored, his straw hat chosen to match. He wore Wolverine work boots that were the same color as his brown leather belt.

The buckle of his belt was large, silver, stamped with a bucking stallion. He looked long, strong, and virile. He looked as if he wanted to snatch her up in his arms and run like hell for the hills.

"No matter what happens," Miranda said, "I'll always be thankful I met you. I'll always remember watching the sun come up in your arms. Everything's been great, Brody. Especially our midnight hour."

A flame of possession smoldered in Brody's eyes, bottomless in their intensity. Leonard might hold the paper to her name, but he held the key to her destiny.

Miranda's heart flipped, her stomach rocked. What if Brody listened to Carmen while she was gone? Then she'd move on, knowing that she'd never find another cowboy to love her the way this man did.

Never.

# Twelve

Brody couldn't stand the suspense. He couldn't stand the uncertainty of knowing if Miranda would come back to him. He couldn't stand doing nothing. Too soon, it was as if their last night together had been too long ago.

He fired off a note to Lillian, written on the back of the grocery list she'd posted on the refrigerator door. He returned the list to the refrigerator, his message short and easy to read:

*Went after Miranda. Call you soon. Brody.*

He threw a bag of clothes and toiletry items together, his spirits soaring from doing something other than brooding over his decision to let Miranda return home with Leonard. He'd been crazy to do that.

He should have gone with her to the hotel where her husband waited for her. He shouldn't have been noble. He shouldn't have let her go. Period.

Just as he gunned his truck off the property, Duke stopped him at the gate. "Just make sure you bring her back." The old man's eyes were bright with speculation. If he could have gone, it was clear he'd have done it. He didn't want to miss the action.

Grinning, Brody hit the road.

So what if he wound up making a fool of himself? He'd feel better knowing he took action to hang on to the woman he wanted instead of sitting at home moping around, hoping she'd call him, hoping he'd made the right choice, knowing in his heart he hadn't.

He couldn't believe he'd been tempted to wait passively while another man decided his fate. Leonard could, right this very minute, be telling any number of lies to keep Miranda back in Tulsa, his private turf.

Miranda had been gone so long she didn't know if Tessa and Leonard were still an item or not. She only had Leonard's word that all she had to do was take care of legal paperwork so they could both be free.

For all Brody knew, she might get to Tulsa and wonder why she'd left in the first place. Her gallery was a hit, the business was bound to be a bigger sensation once she returned to the scene of her crimes.

And to think he'd let her go. This wasn't *Gone with the Wind,* and he wasn't Rhett Butler. He really did give a damn.

Brody intended to be up front and personal, right there in Miranda's face and Leonard's, too. She'd had plenty of time to get her act together on his ranch, time to figure out who she wanted to be with and why.

She'd been right about one thing: He couldn't treat her like a horse or a ranch hand. He couldn't treat her like a lady, either, because ladies didn't take the high road when life wasn't going the way they wanted it to, the way Miranda had done when she left Leonard.

He had to treat her the way she deserved to be treated, as a responsible woman with the guts and drive to stand up for the values she believed in, even if those values were twisted and banged up by personal demons.

Yeah, he thought, she was a little bit on the nutty side, but who wasn't? Carmen had been a rational, loyal friend until jealousy turned her into a scheming, self-serving vixen. Didn't everyone have a line inside them, a line that separated sane, rational choices from the ones that bordered on insanity? He thought so.

Insanity was nothing more than extreme foolishness, like leaving a lucrative, successful horse training operation to chase after another man's runaway wife. It had to be the flip side of walking alone in the dark: Impulsive, irrational, and utterly liberating.

With action, came understanding. He wanted to understand Miranda.

It was going to take him three hours to get to Tulsa, another hour to get his bearings, a quality hotel, directions to Miranda's gallery, her townhouse. He wanted to visualize her world, all of it.

Before he met her face-to-face, shocking her by his arrival, he'd know where Leonard worked, where her parents lived. What he planned teetered on another line, the line of stalking. He was tracking Miranda, scoping out her original territory, intending to steer her back into his personal roundpen.

Never in fifty years would he have imagined himself doing what he was doing right now. He had sixty dollars and some change in his pocket. Crazy. Thank goodness he had credit cards and ATM access.

He'd left home without stopping by the bank or grabbing his checkbook. How many times had Miranda questioned herself once she got started on her self-imposed mission of self-discovery, a discovery that had led her to the point of self-destruction, the point at which he'd found her?

How many times had she wished she'd packed this or that, knowing that she had to make do with whatever it was she had on hand? Brody laughed. Never had he imagined that he'd learn so much about her, after she'd gone.

Only Miranda could determine if she was being stalked or not. This would be decided by her welcome, or lack of it, his willingness to back off, or his unwillingness. The excitement of the unknown boosted his adrenaline. If she told him to get lost, he would, but not until he'd kissed her one more time. If nothing else, he wanted one last kiss.

Oh yeah, Brody thought, as he settled himself comfortably against the bench seat of his king cab, he wouldn't be a fish out of water when he met up with her again. A decisive plan of action required careful thought.

He recalled his conversation with Carmen, words that prompted his decision to go after Miranda. They'd spoken at 9:00 A.M. that morning, Carmen making the first move toward the reconciliation of their friendship.

"I didn't think you'd talk to me, Brody," she said,

her voice a little breathless, a little uneasy over the telephone.

"Can't wipe out a lifetime over one fiasco."

She sighed in relief. "Thank you."

"Don't get me wrong, part of me wishes you hadn't stepped over the line, but that's the smallest part."

"You really do love her, don't you?"

The long night with Miranda had proven at least this much. His feelings for her were genuine, which meant they were made up of everything it took to build a lasting partnership: truth, honor, and communication.

It had taken them all night, but they'd covered the truth through open dialogue. Honor came from doing the right thing on both their parts, her, by returning to Tulsa, him, by letting her go—at least, he hoped he'd made the right choices.

From the moment of Leonard's arrival, Brody's life had been turned upside down. "That's why I'm not steaming anymore. If you hadn't pushed so hard, there's no telling when Miranda's ex-husband would have shown up, if ever. Now, she won't have to duck and hide."

"I tried to look at it from her standpoint," Carmen said, "and when I did, I figured that she hadn't planned on sticking around for as long as she wound up staying. After a while, it had to get harder and harder to come clean. She didn't want to risk losing you."

Brody couldn't believe what he was hearing. Carmen's voice was very sympathetic. "Don't tell me you'd have done the same thing. Not telling me that is."

She made a huffing sound. "I wouldn't have had the nerve to leave town, let alone wander all over the countryside the way Miranda did. I admire that about her, the way she risked it all. That girl ain't even packing a purse. Nope. I couldn't do it."

Brody was too much of a chauvinist to ever truly get a handle on Miranda's willingness to open her life to so much danger. She could have been raped or beaten or murdered, all without being properly mourned. "But for what though? What did she risk?"

"Her art. To find herself. Whatever. Point is, she never would have met you, if she hadn't beat to her own drummer. Got to admire that kind of stick-to-it power."

Tough as he was, Brody couldn't help but appreciate Miranda's sheer strength of will. "I hear you. I don't think I could have done it, either. Just leave everything I know, everything I am behind like that."

"Why not, Brody? Why not just go after her? Why give her ex-husband a second chance to get his act together?"

He didn't pause to think twice about her questions. To him, they were entirely unreasonable. "I have a ranch to run. I can't just pick up and leave."

"What do you think would happen to the ranch if you dropped dead?"

She was one of the few people he knew who spoke to him so plainly. It was one of the reasons he enjoyed their friendship. They were able to talk about most any subject. "Thanks, Carmen."

"I'm serious. The world wouldn't stop. The ranch would go on."

Brody's exasperation showed in his voice. "It's not that simple. I have clients. Meetings. Horses to train."

"Same thing. You're not the only horse trainer in Logan County. You're good, maybe even the best, but you're not the only guy in town. Stay real, Brody. The ranch and everything attached to it would keep on truckin'."

His tone was wry. "Didn't know you were so mercenary."

"I didn't, either. Look, even I can see we'd never work out in the long haul, especially after all this mess with Miranda. Basically, I called to apologize and hopefully figure out a way to still be friends."

"I'm glad you called. We were bound to run into each other again soon anyway. At least the air is clear now between us."

"But," she paused to gather herself, "do you forgive me?"

"Miranda wanted to know the same thing." It was his turn to pause. "Am I really that hard?"

"As in cruel?"

"Yeah. Guess you could put it like that."

"Then, the answer is yes. Once I heard through the grapevine that Leonard Evans had blown into town, I panicked. Let's face it, Brody, what you love, you love, and to hell with the rest of it. You loved Miranda. I wasn't so sure you still loved me—in the platonic sense, of course." The last was said in a rush.

"No. That's not true. Like I said, we can't erase our past."

"I'm one of your oldest friends, right?"

"Right."

"Take it from me, then, you've got a passive-aggressive thing going on. You say you like to go with the flow, but you really don't. You like the safety of routine, the comfort of the same circle of friends. You like what you like and don't go out of your way to change one way or another."

Brody's voice cooled a couple of degrees. "I don't have time for this Cosmo, psychobabble crap, Carmen."

"That's what I mean, hostile. You were all gung-ho to help Miranda, who was nothing more than a stranger in need of a helping hand, but when she stopped fitting whatever image you had of her, you dumped her."

His denial was swift and hot. "I told her to come back if she wants to come back. The choice is hers."

"Some choice. You fought me pretty hard over her, but you let her walk away with her ex-husband, even though she's been hiding from him all this time. I mean, he's not even her ex. He's still the real deal. She was hiding for a reason, but you didn't care about that, you only cared that she, what? Lied to you? Betrayed you? You, the lion-hearted horse whisperer? Mister supposed-to-be-easygoing, but really isn't?"

"Finished?"

"Just getting started."

Brody was determined to hang on to his temper. "I'm not gonna argue with you, Carmen."

"See? There you go with that passive-aggressive, hostile crap. You're mad, but instead of telling me you're mad, you're covering it up with all this coldly polite, don't-want-to-argue-with-you stuff."

"Carmen."

"You can't hide on your ranch and expect life to come to you all the time, Brody Campbell. You've got to grab life sometimes. Get roughed up a little by it. You can't just ease along figuring out other people's—or horse's—problems. You've got to take time for yourself, too. Step out of the box. Go after her."

She'd said an awful lot, and some of it struck home. Miranda had pretty much accused him of the same thought process. "Am I really that rigid?"

"You don't have any major challenges. You've spent your whole life in one place, a place you love and people who love you back. You made the ranch your world. This narrowed your view of everything, even yourself."

His laugh was a low, pensive sound over the telephone wire. She might have been his sister-in-law giving him advice. Instead, she was the dear friend she'd always been, nosey and demanding, always in his corner. "Have you been body-snatched or what?"

"I counsel kids at the high school, remember? I'm only a rodeo queen in my spare time. Go after her, Brody. I'll help Duke and Lillian keep the ranch going. Live your dream. It's what she tried to do."

"What about you?"

"She taught me something, as well."

"What?"

"How to step outside the box. The box is routine. The daily grind. The sameness of who we are and what people expect of us. I always expected you and

me to get together—eventually anyway—and stay
together. Miranda shocked me into realizing I
wasn't really living well. I was just living, hoping for
the impossible."

"Too deep."

"Too real. I love you, Brody. Always will, but like
my girlfriends keep telling me, it's time to move
on."

"Thanks, Carmen."

Her laugh was on the shaky side. They'd crossed
a tremendous hurdle together, each recognizing a
deeper value in the other. "Even for the kick in the
pants part?"

"Perfect timing. And hey?"

"What?"

"Keep an eye out for Genesis."

# Thirteen

Brody found a quality hotel quickly. Within minutes, he'd checked into his garden-themed suite, a comfortable set of rooms designed to service traveling business executives. Everything he needed for comfort and light entertainment was available with ease.

The hotel dining room was three floors down, framed by a courtyard tiled in Spanish ceramic. The ceiling was made of glass, which allowed light to spill over enormous potted plants and trees, many of them tropical.

A waterfall cascaded over rocks and tiny blue tiles, the water a fitting background to the lush greenery everywhere the eye could see. One could spend an entire weekend at the hotel without being bored or tired. The setting was graced with resort amenities.

A woman played the guitar, Ottmar Liebert's *Black Hair in the Wind*. The rumba-styled music worked well with Brody's emotions, high, energetic, specific, and individual. He was free to be himself or someone else.

Is this what Miranda had felt, he wondered, when she stepped away from all she'd known, this liberating sense that all things were possible, if first she believed in herself? She had believed, too, specifically in her art.

Never had she treated her art as a random muse, a skill she couldn't control, one that held her at its mercy. Instead, she had molded her ideas into tangible work, shaped, drawn, painted, and recorded the lost lives of generations of black Oklahomans, those people whose history could easily be forgotten, such as the Abell community where he lived.

In Tulsa, only two people knew his name: Leonard and Miranda Evans. This made him an anonymous figure in the landscape. Anonymous figures blended into the background. In the background, it was easy to observe, listen, and even understand.

This is what he wanted to do, understand precisely what Miranda had given up. He wanted to see through her eyes, walk in her shoes, trace her steps back from his ranch, to her art gallery and townhouse, to her alpha, and her omega.

Those were the only two people who would see him for what he truly was, a man with a subtext to his every conversation. They alone would know that none of his questions were idle, no move careless or uncertain. It was clear that he was in Tulsa to interfere with any situation that might get Leonard and Miranda back together again.

He intended to give Leonard no second chance to rethink his position. After all, Miranda's absence from Tulsa had created a sensation. In her absence, she'd become a trophy wife. The renegade artist's safe capture and return, by her husband, represented a public victory, one that might lead to a private reconciliation.

Leonard was a mercenary, narcissistic man. He

now had two trophies: the baby, which was his whether he married the child's mother or not, and Miranda, an artist whose work was selling faster than it could be created.

Brody had no way of knowing if Miranda, feeling distanced from him, overwhelmed perhaps by the enormity of her return—having to deal with her parents, her staff, her friends, her fans, the media— might hook up with Leonard on the rebound.

Marriage was an intricate, highly emotional, never completely broken relationship. It was never completely broken because memories never die. Brody had to instill new memories in Miranda.

He planned to use the hot tub at the end of his evening. The tub would be a great place to rethink the events that were about to happen next. As he had done in the cab of his truck on the way from Guthrie to Tulsa, he intended to keep his head on tight, through logical thinking and quick action.

Miranda wasn't expecting him. This was good. He hadn't expected her either, and yet she'd wound up altering the course of his life.

Carmen had dropped off two sets of data sheets for him to carry with him on his hero's quest: the documents were the original reports she'd solicited regarding Miranda's background. As was her custom, she'd been thorough.

There were addresses on the reports she provided, hours of operation, names of contact people, such as the manager of the art gallery, including Leonard Evans's secretary at his private psychotherapy practice. His secretary was Tessa Buchanan, Tessa the opportunist, expectant mother of Leonard Junior.

*Action.*

Brody hummed while he showered and shaved: Nothing was impossible.

*Purpose.*

He laid his clothes and accessories out on the bed: Image was everything.

Carefully, he dressed.

He wore a black suede Stetson, a dark blue sweater over a soft white shirt, which he'd tucked into nearly new stonewashed jeans. He wore Sorrell custom boots, soft, supple black ones with silver stitching of horses running.

Every inch of him was lean, hard, and masculine. His mind was focused, his mission clear, to guarantee his future with Miranda. Real cowboys were like salesman, they never gave up and they seldom took no for an answer.

Brody strode through the atrium, tipping his hat at the guitar player, who now serenaded the hotel guests with Ottmar Liebert's *Turkish Night*. A small crowd had gathered to hear her play, the artist with her eyes closed, the artist who played as if there was no one to see the magic wrought by her slender, callused fingers.

Brody, too, had eyes that were blind, only his eyes were blind to the appreciative stares of the women who swept his body with gazes that bordered on lust, and the men who admired his air of rugged, absolute confidence.

He felt marvelous.

# **Fourteen**

Miranda blinked twice when she saw him. On the third blink, she acquired tunnel vision. He was the only thing she could see in a room cluttered with people she wasn't in the mood to know, but had to deal with on a professional level.

Only, she wasn't feeling professional.

Brody moved like a highly developed carnivore, complete with claws, canines, and molars for grasping, ripping, and tearing. He had the fear factor going on, too, a big body of intimidation, a lean human machine equipped with ultrasensitive hearing, acute eyesight, and a primitive thinking process.

Panic seized her, but only for an instant.

He stood out the way a puma would stand out on an urban street corner, this street corner, the site of her one-woman art gallery, more notorious now than ever, because she had once been presumed dead.

Oh, but in Brody's arms, in Brody's territory, she'd been very much alive. She couldn't believe it, that he was here, close enough to see, but not touch. And, dear God, he looked hungry, hungry enough to eat her alive, with or without witnesses.

He might have been lying in wait on her slick

urban street corner, ready to jump his quarry in the
blink of an eye, a flick of the paw. She was that
quarry, she was that prey. No, it wasn't panic she
felt. It was desire.

Being hunted by an old-world cowboy in custom
black boots was entirely inspirational. If she was
feeling the blues before, she couldn't remember
the blues now. Her pulse was ten beats away from
normal it beat so fast.

His being there was incredible, unexpected and
delicious because she'd missed him right after
she'd said the dreaded word good-bye. A split second before leaving, she came close to falling at his
feet to beg him to beg her to stay—but she wasn't
that kind of woman, even if she had to keep reminding herself of that fact.

And here he was, sleek and fit, feline in his big
cat masculinity. She couldn't take her eyes off his
muscles. They rippled and flexed, her tactile memory of them eliciting hot memories of raunchy,
screaming sex, the kind of sex they so recklessly
shared the morning she left his place for Tulsa.

She must have been out of her mind, to leave
him the way she had, with no firm commitment to
return, just a hope, then a prayer. All her business
could have been conducted by mail and by telephone. She hadn't needed to leave Logan County,
but she had, and now she knew why. She had
wanted to test him, see if he really loved her, or the
myth he'd created about her.

The wait had been fraught with tension.

At last, he was here, the man she wanted above
all others, the man who helped her realize how lit-

tle she'd been living, how small and inconsequential her mark had truly been. So what, she was talented, an artist, a painter? There were thousands of talented people in the world.

She had no passion, the real reason she hadn't fought with Tessa for Leonard, or with Leonard to adopt a baby of their own. Brody had opened her heart, which in turn, had made her feel, made her want, made her dream.

Ever since she'd fled Logan County, she'd thought about him constantly, his body, his bed, his lifestyle, with hardly a break to sleep. She continually compared him to every man she met, at the gallery, in the stores, on the drive to her parents' house to reacquaint herself with them and them with her. With Leonard, always with Leonard.

There was no comparison.

They were dynamic men with drastically different styles of being, of thinking, of doing. One man was sexy because he wore his well-spoken, well-read, and meticulous glamour like second skin.

The other man was sexy because he was sex himself—virile, buffed, arrogant, ambitious, superior, and competitive. Brody no more fit into the white-collar world than Leonard fit into blue-collar ranching.

Either man could do it, but he wouldn't be happy.

Brody needed open space, the heat of the sun, the searing cold of winter, all the seasons, every one in its own time. He needed to be close to the land, a man at one with his horse, not a man content to be a spectator from the driver's side of an expensive, highly polished and moving car, a man like Leonard.

No, there was no comparison.

They were distinct species from the same planet. Leonard was the type of man she needed before Tessa Buchanan came along with her scheming ways and her baby-making abilities. He was the kind of man who gave her whatever she wanted as long as she didn't make any waves.

Brody was the man she needed now. To hell with reconstructing the past. The past was gone. Her eyes raked the clothes straight off his back. It was she who stalked up to him. "God, I love you."

He tipped her head into his palm and kissed common sense out the gallery door. He was pure electromagnetic energy. His kiss was a conduit, a facilitator, a connector. That kiss scrawled his name all over her beautiful body, seared his soul all over her talented mind.

It was an exhilarating experience.

He wooed her body and soul with every spiritual cell at his disposal. He had her in his aura, and his aura was her new layer of skin, a skin composed of raw energy, necessary as sex, ethereal as everlasting love, the kind of love poets put into words that live on for centuries, and in this way live on forever.

His aura shimmered, it teased, tempted, and tantalized her. Like the big cat he'd turned out to be, he was too strong and too powerful to be concerned with the curious spectators, the hushed and stunned silence of art gallery patrons who couldn't figure out who in hell he was, or what in hell he was doing with Leonard Evans's wife.

Brody fed his appetite. He wrapped his aura, like jewelry, around the woman who centered his universe. The jewel tones were magnificent: red for power, orange for self-confidence, yellow for stimulation, purple for enlightenment.

He was definitely stimulated. No one knew this more surely than Miranda, his lush, delectable little morsel of love. No way would he let her get away. Not now, not ever. Her hips were pressed tight against him.

Soft. Hard.

Red. Hot.

Unfortunately, Leonard had something to say. "Miranda!" The word came strangled from his throat.

Reluctantly, she let reality bring her back down to earth. After all, the intruder, though estranged, remained her significant other. "Oh," she said, "Leonard."

She met his brutal stare with one of her own. He was supposed to be doing whatever he'd been doing before he found her again, but there he was, reminding her of why she couldn't stand the sight of his face anymore. He wasn't supposed to be at the gallery.

Dressed to kill, he looked neither cool nor collected. He spoke in a tone that was part hiss, part shout. "Have you lost your mind?" He was scandalized. What must people think? What would people say?

She felt like laughing. Hysterically. To think that once she had turned herself inside out for this man. "Have you?"

His manner bordered on violence, as if he might forget where he was, that he had an audience of many, an enemy of one. To the most casual observer, it was clear that Brody wasn't worried about Leonard.

"Don't get smart with me." The warning was clipped short, packed with meaning. Leonard wasn't kidding around, not now, not ever again. It was clear he couldn't wait to be rid of her. She'd made his life a big mess.

The feeling was mutual.

"You don't belong here, Leonard," she said, her attitude one of dismissal. "You never did."

Leonard stabbed a finger in Brody's general, utterly insolent direction. He tried to put words to his emotions, but it had been so long since he'd been jealous about any activity that had to do with Miranda, he wasn't quite sure what to do with himself now that he was rocked with emotion.

Jealous, he fumed, of a cowboy. The man was wearing jeans, not even new ones at that. The man had on . . . the finest custom boots Leonard had ever seen. Damn. Boots like those weren't worn by ordinary men.

Those weren't factory boots with casual leather or assembly line stitching. A man wearing a Seiko Special Agent Man Watch knew all about the tattletale quirks of a man's personal effects. Underneath that high-dollar Stetson was a man of distinction.

But then, even that was too shallow a scratch on the surface of Leonard's surprise, gut-level rivalry. In truth, he was no match for his adversary, a fact that came close to burning a hole in his stomach.

If he'd really been up to snuff, he'd have punched Brody out the minute he'd laid eyes on him when he came through the back door of the gallery. It was as if some primitive intuition had warned him not to come through the front. Something about the front door hadn't felt safe.

There he stood, too, the cowboy, the puma, the predator with teeth slightly bared as Brody coldly calculated his next move. Danger dangled loosely in the air as he tried to decide if he should kick Leonard's ass now or kick it later.

Leonard was so mad he couldn't see the warning signs of his own imminent disaster. "He is the one who doesn't belong here, Miranda," he finally said. "Look at him for crying out frickin' loud! He's the only man here not wearing a suit!"

Her eyes twinkled with all the fresh delight she felt on the inside. Brody was the only person she'd ever met who could throw Leonard off stride. This cowboy turned her lights on. She slapped him on the butt. "Lucky me."

Leonard couldn't breathe, couldn't speak. A vein stood tall on his left temple. His right hand curled into a fist of anger. At the point where adrenaline rushed through his nervous system, poising him for a fight, a man cleared his throat, a subtle form of interruption.

After all, this was a public place.

"Uh," the man said to Brody, "you must be Miranda's new . . . friend." He extended his hand in greeting.

Brody took it, wondering all the while whose side the new guy would take. His, Miranda's, or

Leonard's. He wouldn't be surprised if the very pregnant Tessa was somewhere lurking in the shadows.

The handshake between the men was firm, yet brief.

"I'm Theodore. Miranda's manager here at the gallery. Just call me Theodore. No last name."

Shaved bald, of Samoan decent, Theodore reminded Brody of a volcanic mountain—calm on the outside, but equipped to rumble. Brody liked him on the spot. It helped to see the obvious concern and favoritism he felt for Miranda.

Brody acknowledged Theodore's subtle cues with a polite veneer over his still-ready-to-fight-if-Leonard-wanted-to-fight attitude. "You've done an excellent job here in Miranda's absence."

Theodore smiled at Brody's intelligence. There would be no need for unnecessary roughness, at least not in the gallery. He didn't want to hurt anyone, but he would, if it meant protecting Miranda's physical self or her works of art.

"It was a challenge," he said. "We're getting down to the pen-and-ink sketches. Some of the earlier 3-Ds she'd done. I think people would buy the paint off the walls if we let them."

Leonard's veins were standing out on his neck. How dare they speak as if he wasn't standing there?

HOW.

DARE.

THEY?

"Are you people crazy?" He squealed the words. Several people stepped back.

"Come on, Brody," Miranda said. "Let's get outta here."

Like the prince in her continuing fairytale, Brody swept her up in his arms. He carried her away—to the sound of wolf whistles, cat calls, cheers, and a smattering of romantic laughter. This kind of drama didn't happen every day, especially to the got-money-to-burn crowd that haunted *MIRANDA'S PLACE*.

The pen-and-ink sketches were snatched off easels and marched to the cash register. One more 3-D was plucked off a whitewashed easel on the showroom floor. Conversation roared, the credit card machine ran check after check.

Two sturdy patrons, Theodore's friends, cleverly blocked Leonard's exit so that his wife could escape again.

Leonard was livid.

# Fifteen

They decided on dinner in a gorgeous Italian restaurant not far from MIRANDA'S PLACE. The building was set in the heart of downtown Tulsa, amid commercial businesses and assorted other eateries, and coffee and juice bars.

During the short drive, the couple sat close together, shoulder-to-shoulder on the bench seat, the fragrance of her perfume, Glamorous by Ralph Lauren, drifting between them. In the dim light of early evening, the puma gripped his tender sweet morsel by the hand, and led her into the small restaurant, his makeshift lair.

The restaurant was owned by one of Miranda's friends, Izzy, a Sicilian-born woman of twenty-something who whisked them into a quiet booth near a window overlooking the street. Brody had a clear view of the front door, as well as the restaurant's nearest exits.

If trouble came his way, he'd be ready.

Conversation was minimal as the reacquainting lovers studied the evening's special menu. Brody ordered the same item he ordered whenever he ate Italian, fresh sausage balls and spaghetti. Miranda chose chicken tortellini.

The atmosphere was dark, sensual, the perfect place to air secrets. While the couple awaited the appearance of their main course, wine arrived for their pleasure, as together they savored fresh bread slathered with real whipped butter and nibbled on salad drenched with authentic Italian dressing.

Where once words between them had been many, now there were few. Where to begin? Miranda wondered. Where to begin? Her palms ran slick with sweat. This was her territory, not his, but from the ease in which he sat his chair, he'd taken over.

The flame of an unscented candle flickered between them in a bowl the same shade of red as her lips. Her nails, tipped in the same classic color, reminded Brody of fallen petals, not roses, but the petals of scarlet lobelia as they rested against the thick white linen draped over their dining table.

Exquisite.

The food, the wine, the woman.

Everything.

"I'm glad I came," he said. "Seeing you like this," his eyes poured over the silver and ice dress that poured over her, "is worth a day of my life."

Suddenly, she was nervous, tremulously, treacherously so. Her little laugh gave her away. It was the laugh of a woman certain of the man she loved, but uncertain of her position in his life. "Only a day?"

Brody had no qualms. Sex smoldered beneath the surface of his skin. The aroma of his masculinity escaped the confines of his tightly strummed body, into the air she breathed. Pheromones.

"I'm referring to that dress." His voice made her shiver.

The dress was romantic, feminine in that it accentuated curves once routinely hidden beneath unisex-styled jeans. The soft silk fabric followed the slender lines of her silhouette. She was neither too fat, nor too thin.

She looked healthy.

Her jewelry was as simple as the dress that shielded her naked flesh. She wore a slim gold chain with an amethyst stone around her neck. The stone matched the designs that studded her ears, encircled both her wrists.

He'd never seen her wear jewelry before. Her hair had been freshly done and she wore makeup, skillfully applied. She dressed in the finery and ornamentation she hadn't deemed fit for life on the road.

This meant—she'd been home.

With Leonard, the lying, cheating bastard. Leonard. His nemesis.

Immediately, Miranda sensed the shift in Brody's attitude, but for the life of her, she couldn't figure out what had happened. She was too shy to ask, too conscious of having him near, yet still, so far away.

She cleared her throat. She sipped from her glass. She cleared her throat again. Bottom line, she felt ridiculous. "I keep thinking about Elizabeth Taylor telling Paul Newman in one of their old movies she felt like a cat on a hot tin roof."

No, Brody decided, this would never do.

*Action.*

He signaled the waiter to clear their table. Within minutes, tiramisu arrived, a dessert designed with espresso, cream, and rum. They ate the rich confection with two forks, drank more wine, basked in the smoke filtering candlelight.

Strings and horns and other soothing instruments played over speakers in the background, but neither of them recognized a specific tune other than the fact that the mellow rhythms they heard fit the various degrees of their interlude: Centered, circular, and somber.

They were centered around each other. In this center, there was no past or future, only the present. This was their beginning, the last time they would start over from scratch because this time, there were fewer obstacles between them.

The circle of their oneness remained closed. Whoever entered into this exclusive relationship would be of their mutual choosing. This included family, friends, and colleagues in Tulsa and in Guthrie.

Their attitude was somber. There was still time to quickly follow their new beginning with a permanent and bitter end. Brody didn't believe in begging. He believed in stating his case, hard and thick and possible.

He hadn't driven all the way to Tulsa to leave empty-handed.

In time, and in silence, even their dessert was gone. There was no more wine, only goblets of water garnished with lemon. They needed to press on, otherwise, the evening was a waste of time.

"We can't stall anymore, Miranda."

Her sigh was as eloquent as the love in her eyes. "I know," she said softly. "Where are you staying?"

"Not far from here."

She wasn't surprised. Nothing about him would surprise her anymore. He wasn't just the prince in her fairytale, he was her king. "I can't believe you're here. Theodore said you'd come."

His brow raised in query. "Why is that?"

She traced the stem of her glass with a scarlet fingertip. She'd never noticed how wiry his brows were above his thick, slightly curling lashes. Somehow, she'd become a shadow of a whole woman, and yet, he had seen through her shadows, found the woman she longed to be, not the short-sighted woman she'd become on the run.

Every king deserved a queen, not a princess. He needed to realize how completely ready she was to close the gallery and go home with him to Guthrie. She'd always have ties in Tulsa, but she didn't need to forfeit them in order to build a fresh life with Brody.

She could have it all.

Having it all meant including her closest friends in her new life. These would be the first people to genuinely wish her well. "Theodore figured any man who could make me cry had to be special. I'm staying at his place for now."

Brody took her hands within his own. On close inspection, he spotted blue paint on the flat of her wrist. "I love you, Miranda. I'll always love you."

There it was again, that nervous little laugh.

He frowned when he heard it. Perhaps she wasn't as thrilled to see him as he'd thought she'd be. Perhaps his expectations were just too high. Maybe all the notoriety of her return home wasn't as bad as she'd expected it to be. She had a reputation in either town she'd live in, no matter what she did.

He could deal with her being an outlaw, but could she?

There was only one way to find out. Deftly, he opened the powder keg marked: Danger. "What's wrong?"

How to explain, she wondered, that his being there was like Christmas, only there were fifty boxes to open instead of one. She was overwhelmed, even after the dinner, even under the distant, watchful eyes of her best girlfriend, Izzy.

"I wish," she said, "that we'd done more of this kind of thing back in Guthrie. We didn't go anywhere and yet I was happy."

"We didn't go anywhere because you were hiding."

So, she mused, only the truth would be spoken here. No more games. No more camouflage. He was in command, not she.

The only trouble with this new scenario was that she felt too exposed, vulnerable to the point of not being able to successfully defend herself should things turn nasty before the night was done.

In a fundamental way, Brody was a stranger to her, as she was, in truth, to him. That's why she was hot on the inside, cold on the outside.

"Yes," she said, "That, too. It's no wonder Carmen was so upset. I didn't mix it up with anyone. I mean, I didn't meet your parents."

For the first time since drawing her away from the gallery, Brody drew a curtain over his eyes. He was generous, yes, but he was also possessive. He'd found treasure, secret treasure, and he'd kept it to himself.

"That's because I told them to stay away."

Confusion flickered over her face. Had she been that self-absorbed, that oblivious to all he'd given up to provide her sanctuary? Shame washed over her, stilled the butterflies in her stomach.

"I never knew that."

His shrug was cavalier. He wasn't interested right now in the goings on of Guthrie. "There's a lot about me you don't know. That's why I'm here. I want you to understand that Leonard has no chance of getting you back."

"Leonard can't stand me."

Brody's laugh was deep and masculine. It warmed her cold hands, calmed her skittish heart. Here again was the man who whispered to horses.

"Trust me, Miranda. He wants you. He just can't have you and Tessa at the same time anymore. The baby changed all that."

"I ran into Tessa at the townhouse," she confided.

Aware she was ready to move forward, he encouraged her to continue her confidence. "That must have been awkward."

She leaned back, crossed her legs, drew her hands together in a clasp on the tabletop. "Not really. She said she was sorry."

"How did that make you feel?"

"Free. I mean, there she was, standing in what used to be my living room and I felt sorry for *her*."

"Why?"

"Because I know Leonard. He isn't going to want her to move the furniture or change the kitchen or whatever else because he likes the house the way it is. He tore down my work room and stripped the paper off the walls."

"Ouch."

She leaned forward a fraction, her voice hushed. This man was her friend, her soul mate, and there was no reason she found to pretend that he wasn't. "And you know what?"

"Tell me."

"I stood in my old work room and thought, wow, Leonard Junior is gonna live here, and, well, I wanted him to be happy, Brody. He's innocent of all this nonsense. What better place in my home for him to be than in the room I loved best? Besides, I like to think of it as poetic justice."

"If you're happy, I'm happy."

She hadn't realized the burden she was carrying, the idea she wished Tessa and her baby well. Not many people would believe her; many people would think she was crazy. But Brody understood she'd had enough of pain.

She told him the rest, the part she hadn't yet shared with Theodore, who loved her like a brother, or with Izzy, who loved her like a sister. "I painted a rainbow on the ceiling. Tessa thanked me."

"Women," said Brody, shaking his head in the can't-live-with-them-can't-live-without-them way.

"Yeah, " she said, laughing for real this time. Things were going to be all right. "We're the first ones who go after peace after all the fighting is done."

His grin was a wicked sight to behold. He wanted her clothes off. He wanted her slipping and sliding all over his naked chest. He wanted to work his dinner off, then order more of the delightful Miss Miranda for dessert.

"Speaking of peace," he said, "there's a hot tub in my room at the hotel. Big enough for two."

A glimmer of Miranda-the-daring stared at him right back. She slipped off the silver sandal on her right foot and she slid her scarlet painted toes up his twitching thigh. Her laugh was deep throated and full of her own sensual fire. It was time to exert some control of her own. Every big cat had its mate.

"Come on," she said, "let's get some bubbles first."

The waiter arrived before Brody signaled. The grinning young man dropped a slim, dark burgundy leather portfolio on the white linen cloth that covered their table. The portfolio contained their bill.

But instead of the bill they expected, there was a note. The note read:

*Dinner is on the house.*

# Sixteen

They played in the bubbles until they could scarcely move. All their muscles were relaxed as were their minds. There had been nothing frantic or uncertain about their physical joining, just the sweet satisfaction of knowing they were traveling the same path of discovery together.

Sitting quietly on the small sofa, they refreshed themselves with cold, sweating glasses of bottled water from the convenience refrigerator in the easygoing comfort of Brody's hotel suite.

She wore the one long-sleeved dress shirt he'd packed at the last minute, the tail of it coming to the tops of her bare thighs. He wore a pair of soft blue gym shorts. Both of them were fresh from the shower they'd shared together.

"So," she said, "what did you think of the gallery?"

He considered the elegance of the place, the soft lighting, the top-end clientele, the broad range of work she'd somehow packaged for retail sell. He'd seen the passion she brought to her work by watching her paint at the ranch, but he'd never seen her work in a professional setting.

She was the consummate professional, he decided, elegant, articulate, and clear thinking. It was gratifying to realize she hadn't been solely dependent on Leonard for her financial support or emotional satisfaction.

He smoothed a rough and callused palm over her right thigh. "I hadn't realized the full scale of what you do. For instance, I didn't know you had pen-and-ink drawings in sizes ranging from 3 x 3 inches to 18 x 20 inches."

"That was Theodore's idea," she admitted. "Tourism is big in Tulsa, so travelers are able to take a quality souvenir home with them if they want to. Also, the regular art collector can stock private inventory on a gradual, continual basis. I've gathered quite a following over the years."

"I hadn't expected to see frames hanging from the ceiling."

"We have standard frames for on-the-spot jobs and designer styles for those people who want their work to fit a particular decor. We have a customer who brings color swatches to match frames to her walls at home."

As a man who relied on word-of-mouth for his continued longevity in the business sector, Brody understood the value of customer satisfaction, especially in the simple things. "It helps to diversify."

"It does."

After several moments of companionable silence, Brody put away the small talk and got down to the serious purpose of his romantic quest. "What about the legal work with Leonard?"

Miranda was ready to deal with the tail end of their mutual problem: the permanent separation from her estranged husband. "He'd already taken care of it. I didn't have to do much more than sign on the dotted line."

"Your belongings from the townhouse?"

"Same thing. All boxed up and in my parent's garage. To be honest, I could start over and still not miss that stuff. Traveling the back roads the way I did, with just my backpack, taught me a lot about what's real and what isn't. I'm pretty much a minimalist at this point."

Brody gentled his tone as he broached the next sticky topic. "I bet your folks and other relatives were glad to see you."

"They were," she said, as if she was still surprised by the welcome she'd received. "We had a pretty powerful conversation. They want to meet you."

"Whenever you're ready, I'm ready."

She clasped his hands with her own, then squeezed him as if to reassure them both that the past was truly in the past. "All my business here is pretty much finished. There are no major strings left to cut."

"And the gallery?"

"Theodore will take over the lease. He plans to use the business as a storefront for his boot-making business."

This news threw Brody for a loop as he tried to picture the huge sea islander busy with the detailed artistry required to build boots for a living. He supposed most of Miranda's friends were artists of some kind and that once they made their home together, he'd meet eccentric people more often than he usually did. It would be another way she broadened his worldview.

But still, the idea of the Pacific sea islander stitching delicate designs on boot tops was an incongruent one. "You're kidding?"

Her eyes twinkled. "Scout's honor. We had a pretty decent arrangement hammered out. He worked for me during the day and built boots at night in a crowded storeroom in the back of the business. I got a mostly free employee who doubled as a tough guy on the rare occasions I took my work out for exhibit. He's finally getting a name for himself, and to be honest, we were going to have to do something different anyway."

Brody was reminded of something that struck him as odd at MIRANDA'S PLACE. "No wonder he kept looking at my feet."

"Yeah. It's not often someone walks into the gallery with water buffalo boots on." She couldn't resist flexing her mental muscle on him. She made a game of identifying boot materials whenever she spotted a custom pair.

From the expression on his face, he was impressed. He was really into western attire, and had a huge assortment of sterling belt buckles at home. "How many do you have?"

"No boots. I wear mules that are slip-on shoes, although some people call them cowboy sandals. I've got a kangaroo pair and a set made of calf skin. He makes me purses to match."

Brody pulled her into his arms, marveling anew at the treasure he'd found in her. "I can't believe how much of you I would have missed if I hadn't come here. You've accomplished a lot in less than two days."

"Don't forget," she said, "I've had almost a year to prepare for the grand finale. Leonard and I want this entire episode buried. Whatever doesn't sell before the end of the month will get shipped to me UPS. I figure there's room for one more gallery in Guthrie."

He kissed the top of her tangled hair. "At least one."

She sucked in a huge breath, then let it go in a rush. "I want to give our relationship six months."

"No."

She pulled away in order to scroll his face in consternation. He returned her look with one that said, yeah, you heard right. Still, she said, "Excuse me?"

"You've been on your own for about a year already. You lived under my roof for just about three months, and with my brother before you got to my place. You know who and what I am."

"But, still."

"No buts, Miranda."

"Brody."

He crossed his arms. "Nothing in life is guaranteed. We're young. We have our own professional careers. Neither career interferes with the other. Basically, we have separate, but equal lives. If the relationship works, it works. If it doesn't work, we move on. It's that easy."

He had a point. "What about finances?" she asked.

"The ranch is mine to care for, but I have fifty acres of my own we can build on. That house will belong to us both."

Some of her tension eased away. As he said, there

were no guarantees in life. "You've been doing some thinking, too."

"Every minute since you've been gone."

She gathered her wits and her breath. "Okay, then. Let's go for it."

He pulled her into his arms again, loving the soft warm feel of her, the rightness of his choice. "An artist and a cowboy."

"Carmen will be thrilled," Miranda teased.

"Actually, she will be."

"I was being sarcastic."

"Really. Just like your loyal friends, Izzy and Theodore, I've got loyal friends, too. Happiness and home are where you want them to be, Miranda. I hope you'll remember that when we take off from Tulsa for good."

She pressed her face against his chest. "I just can't believe how smoothly this is all working out."

Brody kissed her forehead, her hair, her cheek, her lips. "We're all responsible adults. Leonard has a reputation and business to manage, just like everybody else. He filed for the divorce, which you didn't contest. We've all got to move on."

"And then there's the baby."

"The catalyst."

"Yes."

He pulled her a little more snug in his arms, as if he'd protect her from every danger or distress if he could. "Do you want a baby, Miranda?"

"I don't know."

He didn't believe her. "You must have felt something specific while you painted that rainbow for Leonard Junior."

She thought a minute. "I suppose what I felt was closure. Some kind of acceptance. I think that's why I painted it so fast. I went there to run through the place one last time and wound up standing in my old work room, thinking, and next thing I knew, I was committed to either continuing my scribble on the ceiling or scratching the project."

"Is that when Tessa showed up?" he asked, trying to establish a sequence of events.

"Oh, yeah. We talked while I painted."

"So you both have closure, then."

"I guess so."

"What do you think Leonard wanted at the gallery tonight?"

"He probably saw the rainbow in LJ's room."

"LJ?"

"That's what Tessa calls the baby. She said having one Leonard around was enough. The gallery was having a special sale that just happened to coincide with my return. Like I said, everything is running so well."

"For you, maybe, but not for Leonard. I think that now that the time is here to burn bridges, he's rediscovering the good parts of your past together. Maybe that's why he went to the gallery."

"I doubt it. He probably wanted to ream me about LJ's room. See, when I paint on the walls, he calls it graffiti."

Brody stared at her a good long while, then he kissed her until she was breathless, until her eyes were trouble free again. "We're going home."

"Now?"

"Now."

She waved a hand at their little trysting spot. Clothes were scattered all over the place. "What about the room?"

"It's a rental. Let's jump in the truck."

When they arrived at the hotel desk, the bill was paid in full. As there had been at the restaurant, there was a note, this one, however, was in a simple white envelope. The note read:

*Campbell,*

*You've got one chance to get this right. Make her happy, or deal with me. I'll be paying a visit.*

*Theodore*

*P.S. The gallery sold out.*

Brody folded the note. He slipped the note in the tight pocket of his stonewashed jeans. If he read the message correctly, Theodore was gonna kick his ass if he broke Miranda's heart.

"What was that all about?" she said.

His grin was a becoming mix of pleasure and pain. "You've got a real knack for picking the best of the best to be your friends."

"What do you mean?"

"Your roommate took care of the bill."

She laughed, caution thrown to the winds of chance, the lure of destiny. "Come on, Cowboy. Let's go home."

# Epilogue

*One Year Later*

Brody sat on the front porch, a glass of tea in his hand. He was staring at the mural she'd painted above the table. In the mural, there was a man and a woman holding hands. In the distance, a horse was breaking free of the barn, his equine friends in tow, a ragtag mix of dogs yapping at them in delight—the games were on.

He couldn't believe how rich his life had become since his marriage to Miranda. There were so many pleasures to enjoy with her, such as beginning and ending his day beside her, naked in bed, holding her, loving her.

He never felt so alive, or so free.

He still didn't believe in guarantees, but he did believe in second chances, that maybe tomorrow things would change and they wouldn't be this happy. Maybe, he thought again . . . tomorrow, but not today.

Miranda came to stand behind him, her arms sliding tight around his waist. "Oh, Brody, our home, everything, is so beautiful."

They had lived in their newly built custom home for three months. Most of the rooms were empty of furniture, the lines of the house simple, every room loaded with light from the many windows which overlooked the property. "It is."

"You think Genesis will ever stop running back to his old stable?"

"Not as long as he can wiggle the lock on his gate."

"Between him and the new foals and whatever else we've got going, time seems to move so fast."

"The gallery is doing well."

"Yeah. Theodore met with Lisa Sorrell the last time he was here. He's thinking about selling some of her custom leather pillows in his shop."

"That would be nice."

"And Izzy says that the next time she takes a vacation, she's staying at our place. She told me to get the guest room finished before summer comes."

"Sounds good to me."

"Brody?"

"Yeah?"

"Ever think what would have happened if I hadn't taken to the road? I mean, it seems like a lifetime ago."

His laugh bordered on the wicked. Turning, he pressed her against his chest. "Carmen might have got her wish."

Miranda smacked him on the butt. "Come on, smart guy, I want to go riding. Let's hit the sheets."

Not needing a second invitation, Brody swung her up into his arms—just as Genesis took off at a run for the home place. "Rain check?" he said.

"Rain check."

And there they lived, together, happily ever after, Sleeping Beauty, and the Prince.

Dear Readers:

You guys are really loyal and I thank you for keeping up with my work. As always, I hope you enjoyed this latest story. I've always considered Logan County a beautiful place to live. Its soil is often hard red clay or fine red sand. There are rolling hills, ponds as large as small lakes, unnamed ravines, myriad creeks and the legendary Cimarron River running through it. The sky is limitless, unbroken by tall buildings and power lines. Nature sounds are constant, noisy, some of them seasonal, all of them comforting. For me, this is home.

Much of the land remains undeveloped. There are native cottonwoods, live oaks, enormous willows, scrubby cedars, redbuds, sweet-tangy honeysuckle, dense thickets of dark berries, tough Johnson grass and gorgeous fields of crayon perfect flowers, a welcome habitat for wild things to find shelter and refuge.

There is no other place I'd rather live. In Logan County, time isn't rushed, it is savored. Neighbors aren't just the people next door, they are people known to you by name, many of them becoming friends. In turn, friends become family. Through family, dreams are lived and shared and sometimes, even conquered.

We often hear of restless, soul-searching men who are rolling stones, but seldom do we hear about women who share this sense of wanderlust. This idea set me thinking about what would it take for a normal, seemingly well-adjusted woman to toss her current dreams to the winds. Would the woman survive, strictly on the most basic levels? Or would she discover the one truth within her character that would heal and sustain her until she defined a new set of goals, a new reality, a new soul? For me, Miranda Evans is such a woman; my mother, Geri, is another.

In the book *Women Who Run with the Wolves,* writer Clarissa Estés speaks of this archetype in fiction literature: the wild woman, *Los Lobos,* or wolf woman. For every such woman, there is a mate, *Mannawe,* the dog man. The dog and wolf are related in context, both tenacious, both survivors, both prepared to live alone or lonely if necessary, but each perceived differently in open society: One is wild by nature. One is tame but shows its teeth. Both are intelligent beings, carnivorous, territorial, and compatible. *Los Lobos,* wolf woman. *Mannawe,* dog man.

In fiction literature, wolves often represent fear, while dogs are billed as man's best friend. If this is true in real life, then it is reasonable to think that wild women inspire fear in the hearts of ordinary men. The ordinary man can crush and squeeze tight a woman's spirit, but the wildness, the original self, the wolf in her, can never be defeated. I used Leonard as the archetype for the ordinary domestic male, Brody as the archetype for *Mannawe,* a man extraordinary in mind and body, therefore worthy of the wild woman who takes him for her own.

I hope you will share your opinion of *No More Tears* with me. There was a time when I answered mail the day I received it, but these days, I get tangled in deadlines and don't return letters as quickly

as I should. Please know that I answer all mail, so
don't think I've forgotten your letter if I take a
while to answer. I can be reached at P.O. Box 253,
Guthrie, OK 73044. Please send a SASE with your
letter. I save and cherish every one I receive.

My best to you always,
Shelby